LESI   many
awa   *lyphics,*
co-a   for the
CB.   A Book
of t   *ver,* the
firs   Cylinder
Aw   k of the
yea   he CLA
You   Award.
Liv

Jor   *Curse in*
Hi   own for
bei   ationally
bro   7, where
he routinely found himself in close contact with major
science fiction and fantasy stars, and was a voice for
genre fans everywhere. Llyr continues to write and act in
film and television. He lives in Toronto.

THE WIGGINS WEIRD · BOOK 2

THE HAUNTING OF HECK HOUSE

LESLEY LIVINGSTON AND **JONATHAN LLYR**

STORYBOARD ILLUSTRATION BY STEVEN BURLEY

PUFFIN
an imprint of Penguin Canada Books Inc., a Penguin Random House Company

Published by the Penguin Group
Penguin Canada Books Inc.
90 Eglinton Avenue East, Suite 700, Toronto, Ontario, Canada M4P 2Y3

Penguin Group (USA) LLC, 375 Hudson Street, New York, New York 10014, U.S.A.
Penguin Books Ltd, 80 Strand, London WC2R 0RL, England
Penguin Ireland, 25 St Stephen's Green, Dublin 2, Ireland (a division of Penguin Books Ltd)
Penguin Group (Australia), 707 Collins Street, Melbourne, Victoria 3008, Australia
     (a division of Pearson Australia Group Pty Ltd)
Penguin Books India Pvt Ltd, 11 Community Centre, Panchsheel Park,
     New Delhi – 110 017, India
Penguin Group (NZ), 67 Apollo Drive, Rosedale, Auckland 0632, New Zealand
     (a division of Pearson New Zealand Ltd)
Penguin Books (South Africa) (Pty) Ltd, 24 Sturdee Avenue, Rosebank,
     Johannesburg 2196, South Africa

Penguin Books Ltd, Registered Offices: 80 Strand, London WC2R 0RL, England

First published 2014

1 2 3 4 5 6 7 8 9 10   (WEB)

Copyright © Lesley Livingston and Jonathan Llyr, 2014
Illustrations copyright © Steven Burley, 2014

Manufactured in Canada.

LIBRARY AND ARCHIVES CANADA CATALOGUING IN PUBLICATION

Livingston, Lesley, author
    The haunting of Heck House / Lesley Livingston and Jonathan
Llyr ; storyboard illustration by Steven Burley.

(The Wiggins weird ; book 2)
Ages 8 and up.
ISBN 978-0-14-318426-3 (pbk.)

I. Llyr, Jonathan, author II. Burley, Steven, illustator III. Title.

PS8623.I925H39 2014   jC813'.6   C2014-904436-4

eBook ISBN 978-0-14-319319-7

Visit the Penguin Canada website at **www.penguin.ca**

Special and corporate bulk purchase rates available; please see
www.penguin.ca/corporatesales or call 1-800-810-3104.

FOR SIMON EVANS. MAN.
MACHINE. DRIVE—INSPIRATION.

CONTENTS

1 IT CAME FROM THE THIRD DIMENSION!

"I wouldn't go in there if I were you ..." Tweed Pendleton murmured in a gravely singsong monotone.

"Save your breath, pal," Cheryl Shumacher whispered breathlessly. "They are *totally* going in there."

"They never learn."

"They never do."

The two girls—both twelve years old, cousins and best friends—watched the action unfold on their beloved Drive-In movie screen as Freddy and Marlene, a young, dewy-eyed, newlywed couple, decided *not* to turn around and leave the attic of the creepy old house they'd only just bought as a fixer-upper. Even though the storm raging outside had knocked the power out and the flashlight in young Freddy's hand was running low on juice, they weren't leaving.

After all, they'd already completely ignored the inexplicable warnings of "Get out!" and "Don't go in the attic!" that kept appearing in bathroom-mirror fog and splattered in ketchup on the kitchen walls.

Near giddy with excitement, Cheryl and Tweed kept their eyes glued to the screen.

Creeeeeeeaaaakkk ... The attic door slowly opened. Freddy's watery flashlight beam swept the shadowy gloom.

"See, honey?" he said. "Nothing to worry ab— AAAGGHHH!!"

"EEEEEEEKKKK!!!" Marlene shrieked in terror.

Ghostly, skeletal hands reached right out toward Cheryl and Tweed, seeming almost to brush within inches of their faces before wrapping around Freddy's arms. The malevolent spirit of Old Lady Brakenbiscuit screamed in hysterical triumph and dragged poor Fred into the darkness as the attic door slammed shut and Marlene tore down the staircase, out the front door and ran for her life!

Cheryl and Tweed laughed, toasting each other with their chocolate-dipped ice cream cones and shovelling more popcorn into their mouths with contented sighs. Their sage advice had once more been ignored and they couldn't be happier. Cheryl Shumacher and Tweed Pendleton had dedicated their young lives to watching movies (particularly B-grade ones), studying the teachings of the silver screen, learning its lessons, listening to its wisdoms and living their lives according to its hidden truths. High up on that list of truths, of course, was "Don't go up into a creepy old attic during a thunderstorm."

Cheryl pushed her cardboard 3D glasses up her nose with one knuckle so they fit more securely on top of her own regular glasses.

"Thank goodness they never learn!" she said, her braces creating a hint of a lisp. "If they did, we wouldn't have had such an embarrassment of riches to choose from for this awesome-tastic triumph of three-dimensional double-bill programming."

"You got that right," Tweed agreed in her signature monotone and pointed at the screen. "Oh good— look—Marlene is out in the yard running straight for the abandoned caretaker's shack where all those rusty old garden tools are stored."

Cheryl and Tweed had been given the duty of choosing what movies would go on the weekly double and triple bills for the Starlight Paradise Drive-In Double-Screen Movie Theatre by their grandfather Jefferson "Pops" Pendleton, only a week earlier. This was their second effort and it had been a hard choice to make. Thematically, they'd decided early on to go with ghost stories. That was the easy part. But there were so many gems to choose from!

Should they go for the funny? Like, say, *The Ghost and Mr. Chicken* (classic Don Knotts fare, complete with goofy faces and funny voices). Or, perhaps, the campy? Like, say, the Ed Wood–directed low-budget classic *Night of the Ghouls*, with its floating-sheet ghosts and truly bizarre seance scene attended by skeletons and complete with a hovering trumpet? Or should they just go straight for the terror? Like, say, *Seance in Suite 777*. Or *Sleepover Slaughter* ... Or even the offbeat? Like, say, *Spookapalooza*—a '90s grunge-era pic, shot handheld-style like a documentary of a music festival, but on ancient burial grounds.

The girls had wanted quality—they had both immediately rejected the box-office flop *Don't Turn Around!* along with its even floppier sequel, *No, Seriously, Don't Turn Around!* Also the less-than-B-grade efforts *This Ghoul's for Hire*, *Ghost with the Most*, *Moon over Splatter Manor* and *Shriek Shack*. Those movies were all overstuffed with characters they called, "Too Stupid to Live" (or TSTL for short). No, the girls valued the intelligence and discerning tastes of their prospective patrons.

Ultimately, they'd gone with truly timeless fare for their double bill: the classic haunted mansion picture *Menace of Maison de Casa House*, followed by the horror-comedy masterpiece *Ding Dong, You're Dead!*

And the icing on the ghoulish cake? Both pictures were available in 3D! Cheryl and Tweed had been dying to hand out the cardboard green-and-red-lensed 3D glasses, which had been languishing forever in a box on a shelf in the projection booth, to the Drive-In's patrons, and finally this was their chance! The town of Wiggins Cross would be abuzz on Monday morning with water-cooler movie chat!

Now, as they sat in Pops's pickup truck at the back of the Starlight Paradise's (full-to-capacity, thanks to their excellent choices) Drive-In movie lot, the girls revelled in the squeals of gleeful terror that occasionally drifted over from the other cars parked in the lot. Every time a ghostly hand or ghastly face or—as in the scene they now watched, wide-eyed—floating garden implement seemed to leap off the screen and through the windshields of the parked cars, the girls could see the vehicles shudder with the responses of their occupants. And they would trade worldly glances, knowing that—although enjoying their audiences' reactions—they, themselves, were far too steeped in the traditions of the cinema to ever fall for the sudden-shock scare.

"Amateurs," Cheryl said. "Nothing scares us."

"Oh, absolutely." Tweed nodded, her solemn grey eyes unblinking behind the parti-coloured 3D lenses. "Nothing in the world could possibly—GAH!!"

The inside of the truck cab suddenly exploded with snacks as a ghastly creature leaped up from right in front of the front bumper, landing loudly on the hood and, contrary to the girls' recent assertions, scaring the ice-cream-loving socks right off both of them! Cheryl's double-dip ice cream wound up stuck to the roof of the cab when she launched it into the air in involuntary terror. The cracked cone dripped ice cream onto her freckled nose. The fringe of Tweed's straight, dark hair had lost some of its gothy seriousness, dotted as it now was with gummi worms and popcorn puffs. Beneath the fringe, her 3D glasses sat askew at a hilarious angle.

Outside, on the hood of the truck, their grandfather Pops laughed as he pulled the inside-out clown mask off his head, pleased that he had once again managed to startle his unstartleable granddaughters. The girls had to give him credit. His usual methodology was to wait until they had been lulled deep into their movie-watching groove, then he would climb quietly up into the truck bed and—during a suspenseful scene—pound on the roof of the cab. This time, Cheryl and Tweed had secretly rigged up fishing line tripwires connected to jingle bells in the cab so they'd be alerted to his approach. But Pops had been on to their booby trap and, sneaking around to the front of the old pickup, had made good use of the 3D effects emanating from the big screen.

"Well played, Pops," Cheryl murmured, plucking her ice cream stalactite from the ceiling and plopping its sticky remains into her empty soda cup.

"Well played, indeed," Tweed agreed, untangling a gummi worm from her bangs.

Still chuckling, Pops came around to the driver's-side window, where the car speaker, removed from its resting post, hung inside. He knocked a knuckle on the glass pane. Tweed rolled the partially open window down far enough for Pops to stick his head inside the truck.

"Picture's over in fifteen minutes, girls," he said. "I expect you both to be in bed with your teeth brushed and PJs on right after the end credits roll, all right?"

"Okey-doke," Cheryl said.

"Affirmative." Tweed nodded.

"That's my girls," Pops said and wandered back toward the Drive-In's Snak Shak.

The girls had lived with their grandfather in his farmhouse at the edge of the Drive-In lot ever since they were five years old. Everyone in Wiggins referred to them as "the twins" and they were, in fact, identical twins—just not with each other. They were cousins. But one day seven years earlier, on a double family outing, Cheryl and Tweed and their twin sisters and parents had all boarded a small plane and headed out for a weekend vacation in the mountains west of Wiggins.

That was the last anyone saw of Cheryl's family, or Tweed's family, or the family friend who had piloted the plane. Cheryl and Tweed were found alone in the foothills two days later, unharmed but with no recollection of what had happened beyond a flash of bright white light. No one in Wiggins liked to talk much about "The Incident," but, whatever had happened all those years ago, it had forged an unbreakable bond between the cousins. Well, that ... and a mutual love of B movies and buttered popcorn. Along with a burgeoning babysitting business!

As Pops ambled off, the girls braced themselves for the movie's big finish—wherein the clueless couple, Freddy and Marlene, hire a wacky mystic who holds a seance to rid the house of its wicked ways and evil attitude. Only, of course, to have the whole thing spectacularly backfire with huge amounts of supernatural fireworks and running and screaming as the old film fades to the end credits. Giggling and satisfied, Cheryl and Tweed punched each other in the arm.

Another successful movie night at the old Drive-In.

After the flick, the girls took a bit of a detour on the way to the white farmhouse they called home, bypassing the Drive-In's mini-putt range and swinging by the big old red barn—which housed C+T headquarters—to drop off their 3D glasses, customized with sparkle stickers and glitter glue, and stash their favourite movie-watching blankets and pillows.

They were on their way out of the barn when they caught sight of a small square envelope, lying on the floor just inside the barn door.

"Hey! Look at this!" Cheryl bent down to examine the rather fancy-looking stationery illuminated by a single shaft of moonlight. The envelope was made of heavy, cream-coloured paper with a ruffle-edged flap. Inside was an antique-looking formal invitation.

Tweed leaned over Cheryl's shoulder as she read the precise, elegantly embossed, gold lettering.

An OPEN INVITATION to
the Notable Young Sitters of
WIGGINS CROSS

You are hereby invited
to a friendly overnight competition—comprised of skills
challenges—for the purpose of determining who is best
suited to be awarded a contract to
House-Sit
at the noble and prestigious
residence of
Sir Hector Hecklestone the Third,
while his Lordship and Family travel abroad.

Please present yourselves, along with this invitation,
at sundown, tomorrow eve.

44678 Eerie Lane, Wiggins Cross

H. H. III

Participants must be 13 years of age or older.

"Holy moly!" Cheryl exclaimed. "This could be our ticket to the big time!"

"Oh, absolutely." Tweed nodded vigorously. "Our sitting skills are honed. Razor sharp. Especially after the carnival incident and the addition of our pet-minding services par excellence."

The girls grabbed hands and began to jump around the barn in a crazy little dance of super-sitter glee.

A week earlier, a travelling carnival had set up shop—or, rather, tents—in the empty field across the road from the Drive-In, and through a series of unfortunate events had unleashed a cursed mummy princess on the unsuspecting Wiggins folk. Thanks to the timely intervention and curse-foiling pizzazz of Cheryl and Tweed, along with their best friend, Yeager "Pilot" Armbruster, and their ten-year-old nemesis-turned-trusty-sidekick, Artie Bartleby, the town was saved. All this had happened at the same time as the girls had been engaged in cat-sitting fifteen—*fifteen!*—furballs for the town's middle school librarian, Marjorie Parks.

"I'll bet you Miz Parks has been chatting up friends and acquaintances," Cheryl surmised, slapping the stiff paper invite in the palm of her hand. "No doubt regaling them with tales of our superior customer care and the overall satisfaction of her passel of puddins."

"No doubt," Tweed agreed. "Word of mouth is a powerful marketing tool. And our new flyers and capital

W-O-W slogan branding should get us some serious sitter traction."

W-O-W stood for "While-O-Wait." The slogan had started life as a typo on Cheryl and Tweed's business cards—the girls took their fledgling sitter business very seriously—and had been meant to read "While-*U*-Wait" but instead had come back from the printer reading:

Cheryl & Tweed's
Expertitious Child-minding Services
(and Auto-vehicular Detailing)
While - O - Wait

Instead of correcting the glitch and shelling out allowance money for another print run, the twins had embraced the quirky phrase and used it as both a catchy (if somewhat nonsensical) slogan and motivational expression.

"Totally," Cheryl said, in answer to Tweed's assertion. "Odd to think that, in light of all that, this Sir Heck-en-whatzits fellow wouldn't just offer us the contract right off the bat."

"Sure," Tweed said. "Although, to be fair … I don't remember delivering any flyers to anywhere on that street."

"Good point. In fact, *I'm* not even sure I know where that street is."

Tweed trotted over to the work table on the other side of the Moviemobile, a 1964 Mercury Comet convertible with an old TV bolted to the hood and a VHS player retrofitted under the dash (perfect for movie watching on the nights when the Drive-In was dark), and fished through a stacked pile of envelopes and papers, looking for a map of the town of Wiggins Cross. The girls had been using it to plan their flyer routes and distribute freshly printed info sheets in the wake of their successful retrieval of a quartet of escaped toddlers—the Bottoms boys—advertising a one-time-only discount for new clients. Never mind the fact that the very next day the girls had then had to rescue the boys from an ancient curse that had transformed them into the reptilian minions of an Egyptian mummy princess. In the end, disaster had been averted and Mr. and Mrs. Bottoms had been none the wiser.

Of course, Cheryl and Tweed hadn't been able to use any of that in their promotional material. But they'd been buoyed by their successes nevertheless, and it had spurred their advertising efforts. They must have stuffed fifty mailboxes with flyers. At least. Maybe this Hecklestone House had been one of them.

After a few moments of paper shuffling, Tweed found what she was looking for and spread the map out on the work table, smoothing down the creases and flattening the edges. There were marks on the map made in neon marker—streets and neighbourhoods circled and crossed off—all places where the girls had covered territory in their bouts of flyer blitzing. Which meant that, with the exception of the downtown business district and a somewhat industrial zone on the eastern edge of town, most of the map was a brightly coloured patchwork.

"Eerie ... Eerie ..." Tweed muttered, running her finger in a zigzag pattern from side to side across the town's contours. "I don't see any—wait! Here it is ... Eerie Lane."

"Lessee!"

Cheryl leaned on her elbows over the map and looked at where Tweed's finger pinned the paper. She blinked, not certain what her cousin was pointing to, at first. But then, sure enough, there was a line—barely more than a half-inch squiggle—that branched off at a right angle about three-quarters of a mile down past where Rural Route #1 crossed a dilapidated old covered bridge on the western edge of town. It was well within bike-riding distance, and yet the girls had never encountered the little street. Maybe it was because that particular bit of map seemed ... faded. Foggy. Just a bit out of focus compared to the crisp lines that criss-crossed the rest of the paper's surface. Probably a printing error.

"Well, I'll be danged," Cheryl murmured. She straightened up and blew a strand of twisty strawberry-blonde hair out of her eyes. "I have to admit, I am intrigued."

"Intrigued enough to take the night off from our usual movie watching?" Tweed asked.

"A sacrifice to be sure, but one I feel we should make, under the circumstances," Cheryl said in all seriousness.

"Oh, definitely." Tweed nodded. "We are, after all, seekers of the unknown."

"You got that right, partner. And it's kinda, I dunno, refreshing to know that there are still unknowns to be known in a place like Wiggins."

"The mysteries of the universe unfold before us."

"Tomorrow first thing, we'll get our sitter gear together and prepare to embark on this new adventure," Cheryl said, stifling a yawn. "While-O-Wait!"

"W-O-W, indeed," Tweed said with satisfaction. "That old Heck House won't know what hit it!"

2 IT CAME FROM THE FOURTH DIMENSION!
(PREVIOUSLY TITLED: IT CAME FROM THE THIRD DIMENSION 2)

Preparations for the House-Sitter Smackdown Extravaganza were necessarily delayed the next morning when the girls found a note on the refrigerator door from their grandfather. Pops had risen early and was out in the far Drive-In lot, busy repairing one of the movie projectors for the Starlight Paradise's second screen. About a year earlier, a ferocious lightning storm had zapped the projection booth, causing the projector to blow a gasket, and Pops had been looking around for new parts to repair it. Because it was an older machine, his search wasn't an easy one, but he'd finally tracked down all the doohickeys that he needed. In the note, Pops mentioned that he'd enlisted the help of the twins' best friend, Pilot, who was handy with tools and fixing stuff. (Pilot's dad had been the one flying the plane that had disappeared with Cheryl and Tweed's families, and he'd inherited an old crop-duster that was forever in need of tinkering and tune-ups, so the twins knew he'd be more than happy to lend a hand.)

Pops asked if, in the meantime, the girls wouldn't mind taking care of another Drive-In maintenance issue. Seemed that a patron had complained—on the second night of Cheryl and Tweed's first-ever programming stint, a triple bill of creature movies—that his in-car speaker had been malfunctioning. Seeing as how the first night had been cancelled because everyone in town had gone to the carnival across the road, the girls were keen on optimizing all future movie-going experiences for their patrons, and so they hopped right to the task of hunting down exactly which speaker out of over a hundred in the lot was out of kilter.

Cheryl stood, fists on her hips, and gazed out over the vast sea of metal boxes perched on poles. "Huh. So. Which one d'you think it is?" she asked Tweed.

Tweed's grey eyes narrowed as she contemplated the question. "Could be any one of 'em ..." Not about to be daunted by the potentially day-devouring task set before them, she shrugged one shoulder and cocked her head. "Maybe we should spice up the job with a good old-fashioned round of ACTION!!"

Cheryl nodded enthusiastically. "Capital idea!" she said.

ACTION!! was a favourite game of make-believe

the girls were fond of playing when faced with a tedious or difficult task. In ACTION!! mode, the twins were no longer small-town girls in a small-town world, but larger-than-life heroes living lives of high adventure. They could see it all—just like a movie storyboard! And hear it all—just like dialogue from a movie script!

With a bit of pre-chore preparation, along with a healthy dose of imagination (which the twins were in no short supply thereof) and a few "magic words," the Great Speaker Hunt was on! The girls exchanged their C+T Secret Signal (patent pending), which consisted of one winky eye, a pointing index finger pressed against the side of the nose and a firm nod.

"Cameras rolling ..."

"Aaaaand ..."

"... ACTION!!"

**EXT. TEMPLE RUINS IN A JUNGLE SETTING --
MORNING**

CAMERA PUSHES IN SLOWLY toward a pair of
FEMALE FIGURES, laden with gear, creeping
cautiously toward an ELABORATELY CARVED STONE
ARCHWAY, the entrance to a VINE-SHROUDED
ANCIENT TEMPLE. The only sounds heard are
nervous BIRDSONG and the eerie whispering of
tropical LEAVES.

> TREASURE HUNTER TEE
> Looks like this could be the
> place ...

> TREASURE HUNTER CEE
> Gotta be. I don't see any other
> cursed ceremonial Aztec temples in
> this here neck o' the jungle.

CLOSE-UP ON: a TATTERED MAP held in a pair of
steady hands. There is a dotted line leading
to an ominous SKULL-MARKS-THE-SPOT.

CAMERA RISES up from map to a TWO-SHOT of
our heroes: A PAIR OF WILY TREASURE HUNTERS,
dressed in adventurer-practical ensembles.

> TREASURE HUNTER TEE
> The resting place of the *Idol of
> Speak-El-Speak-Quel*, Voice of
> the Vengeful Gods, Keeper of the
> Starlight Secrets, Protector of the
> Paradise --

                    TREASURE HUNTER CEE
                      (impatiently)
         Yeah, yeah. All that stuff. Let's do
         this thing -- and remember -- no one
         has ever come out of there alive ...

They step through the archway. Camera
pans FULL-CIRCLE to show the INTERIOR OF
THE TEMPLE. The STONE PASSAGE is a MAZE,
festooned with VINES that criss-cross the
open space like spiderwebs. IN THE SHADOWS,
the treasure hunters can see DOZENS OF IDOLS,
ALL IDENTICAL, GLARING AT THEM.

They are EXTREMELY MENACING.

                    TREASURE HUNTER TEE
         Decoys! Which one is it? Which one is
         the real idol?

                    TREASURE HUNTER CEE
                 (eyes scanning the sea of idols)
         That one!

HUNTER CEE points at one particular idol, set
somewhat apart from the rest. It has a jewel
set in its forehead that seems to be faintly
GLOWING.

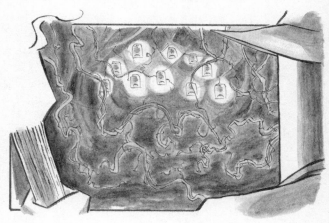

She takes a confident step forward, steps
on a VINE and triggers a BOOBY TRAP! A JET
OF DEADLY ACID sprays just in front of her
as HUNTER TEE grabs her jacket and yanks her
back.

                    TREASURE HUNTER CEE
                         (shaken)
          Thanks, partner. Uh ... Don't step on
          the vines.

                    TREASURE HUNTER TEE
                 (also shaken, but better
                       at hiding it)
          Right. Good plan. Stay alert. No
          telling what else this place has in
          store for us.

MULTI-SHOT SEQUENCE of the HUNTERS
acrobatically dodging and ducking the network
of VINES.

As they approach the STONE ALTAR where the
IDOL hangs from a hook on a carved post,
HUNTER CEE accidentally snags her PICKAXE
on a TRIP VINE ...

This TRIGGERS A VOLLEY OF POISON ARROWS!!

The HUNTERS make a RUN for it ...

Only to have a GAPING CHASM open in the
stone floor between them and the ALTAR!

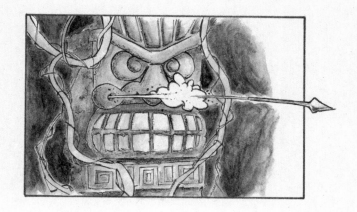

In desperation, THEY LEAP!! ...

GRASP the crumbling stone ledge ...

And SCRABBLE up the rock face to RELATIVE
SAFETY ...

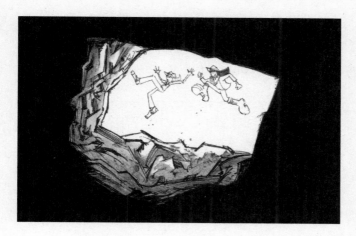

CAMERA ZOOMS IN on their wide-eyed reactions.

> TREASURE HUNTER CEE
> (panting)
> Well ... okay then ... there's my
> calisthenics for the day ...

> TREASURE HUNTER TEE
> (gasping)
> Oh ... sure ... good exercise. All in
> a day's treasure hunting ...

The HUNTERS clamber unsteadily to their feet
and turn to face the IDOL. The little stone
head of the SPEAKER GOD glares at them.

The HUNTERS circle around to opposite sides
of the altar post.

HUNTER CEE pulls a PUTTER from a holster on
her back and sights down its length. HUNTER
TEE produces a CATCHER'S MITT and assumes
a ready stance. HUNTER CEE squints, leans
forward and lines up the golf club like a
pool cue, aiming it at the IDOL ...

                    TREASURE HUNTER CEE
                (tongue stuck out one side
                       of her mouth)
          Ooookay ... Idol in the corner
          pocket ...

She knocks the IDOL from its perch ...

Right into HUNTER TEE's catcher's mitt!
PERFECT SHOT!!

There is a FROZEN MOMENT OF SILENCE. The two
HUNTERS grin at each other ... and then ALL
HECK BREAKS LOOSE!!!

The temple VINES start to SNAP and WHIP
AROUND! DARTS and ARROWS zip through the air!

The HUNTERS cover their heads, leap back over
the chasm and run recklessly for the exit in
a ZIGZAG pattern ...

SUDDENLY, the HUNTERS hear a THUNDEROUS
RUMBLING coming from RIGHT BEHIND THEM!
They look back to see ...

They are being CHASED BY AN ENORMOUS ROCK,
CARVED IN THE SHAPE OF A SACRED AZTEC MINI-
DONUT!!

The HUNTERS barrel through the ARCHWAY and
land in a heap.

Suddenly, the IDOL's RUBY EYE GLOWS TO LIFE
and a DISEMBODIED VOICE CRACKLES out of
SPEAK-EL-SPEAK-QUEL!

                    SPEAK-EL-SPEAK-QUEL
                       (angry and staticky)
          Great Houdini's Hot Pants! What
          the -- who the -- unhand me, you
          urchin!!

                    TREASURE HUNTER CEE
                          (startled)
          Gah!

                    TREASURE HUNTER TEE
                       (even more startled)
          GAH!! Cut!! CUT!!!

"CUT!! ..."

"Cutting! Cutting!" Cheryl yelled frantically in answer to Tweed's equally frantic direction. The ACTION!! sequence came screeching to a halt as the girls froze. After a moment, Cheryl's pigtails—strawberry blonde and sprouting askew from both sides of her head—bounced furiously as she whipped her head around, searching for the source of the voice she and Tweed had just heard. Tweed on the other hand, didn't move. She just stood there, staring with wide grey eyes at the battered rectangular-shaped metal box, cradled in the catcher's mitt she held in both hands. Her arms were stretched so far out in front of her, she looked as if she was trying to back away from them. Or from the object that had just squawked at them in an outraged, slightly nasally English accent.

"What the ...?" Cheryl stepped forward and peered closely at the Drive-In car speaker as if it were an alien life form. Intriguing, but not to be trusted. She glanced back up at Tweed. "Did that thing just say something?"

Tweed nodded silently, clearly more freaked out by that fact than she was comfortable with.

"Maybe Pops is testing the system," Cheryl suggested. "Maybe—"

She snapped her jaw shut when the reason for Tweed's freaked-out-ishness became apparent as she juggled the catcher's mitt slightly so Cheryl could see the bottom of the speaker. The thing was—at least it *should* have been—totally defunct. Trailing from the metal housing were two wires with frayed, frazzled ends. It happened occasionally—the local squirrel population wasn't that bright and were prone to chewing through things they had no business chewing through—but, because of that, there was no possible way that speaker was still hooked in to the Drive-In system. And that wasn't the only thing. It also sported what, at first, seemed to be a round red indicator light bulb on top—the "jewel of Speak-El-Speak-Quel." In their ACTION!! game, that hadn't seemed so odd. Only, in real life ... well ... the Starlight Paradise Drive-In movie theatre in-car speakers *didn't* have indicator light bulbs on top.

"Um ..." Cheryl leaned forward—just a bit—and stared at the thing.

"You heard that," Tweed said. "Right? You heard it talk?"

Cheryl nodded vigorously and went back to staring.

"Take a photograph!" the speaker suddenly exclaimed in an annoyed tone, the red light pulsing in time to the words. "It'll last longer!"

"Gah!"

Both girls screamed and Tweed jumped, involuntarily launching the speaker into the air.

"GAH!!" the speaker screamed back as it flew in an arc. And then, "Ow! Ow! Ow!" as it bounced along the hard-packed ground. "Ow ..." When the speaker came to rest against a raised clump of crabgrass, the light dimmed and the voice moaned softly to itself.

Tweed glanced around wildly to see if anyone was nearby. The coast was clear. With Cheryl standing by, muscles tensed and ready to provide any necessary backup, Tweed tiptoed toward the groaning, inert speaker. From a distance of three feet, she pounced and landed on the thing, trapping it beneath her catcher's mitt.

The speaker squealed and hissed in tinny-sounding, electronic rage.

"Unhand me!" it cried, crackling loudly from beneath the worn leather mitt. "Where am I? What's going on?"

Tweed leaped backward through the air like a startled grasshopper. Her gothy footwear—big black boots with lots of buckles—tangled in the skipping-rope vines and upended her. She landed nose-to-nose with the speaker, her big grey eyes wide.

"Did … um. Did you say something?" she asked, her usually solemn tones gone a bit squeaky from astonishment. "Mister … um … Speaker?"

There was a faint sound of static.

Tweed tentatively reached out and plucked up the end of the wire.

Cheryl crouched down and examined it closely. It looked as though it had suffered a miniature explosion. The hole in the speaker housing where the wire attached was blackened with scorch marks. Cheryl poked the thing with one finger.

"Hey! No poking!"

The twins exchanged a look. Then Cheryl glanced around the Drive-In lot to see if anyone was nearby. Maybe Pilot was joking around and trying to scare the girls. But no. Pilot was nowhere in sight. And so, clearly, not playing some kind of practical joke.

The lot was deserted.

"Dudley?" the speaker asked suddenly. "Is that you? Dudley!"

Cheryl and Tweed both jumped at the sound of that name and shared an alarmed glance. *Dudley?* The only Dudley the girls knew was the shady carnival owner, Colonel Winchester P.Q. Dudley, whom they'd had a hand in running out of Wiggins only a few days earlier. And, frankly, the girls were still in a bit of shock that they'd gotten away with such high-adventure monkey-shines without their beloved grandfather discovering their secret and grounding them for life. So, really, it wouldn't do to have Pops's own Drive-In equipment spouting the name of Cheryl and Tweed's nefarious nemesis at the top of its lungs.

Not ... that it actually had lungs.

Or a brain.

Or any capacity, really, to be speaking on its own in any way.

It had to be some kind of a trick.

But a trick that was going to land the girls in a hea of trouble if they had to explain it to Pops Pendlet Cheryl and Tweed had made the decision not to tell about the carnival/mummy princess shenanigans, and Pilot and Artie Bartleby had heartily agreed to keep the whole adventure under wraps.

Wiggins folk already regarded the "twins" with some skepticism. Long ago, in the days following "The Incident," people in the town had been convinced that the Shumacher/Pendleton/Armbruster disappearance was due to some sort of unfortunate accident. The girls had developed ideas of their own—*alien* ideas—and, at first, the Wiggins folk had indulged them. After all, they'd been very young. But when the passage of time did little to lessen the twins' growing certainty of paranormal meddling, and their developing obsessions with B movies began to colour their increasingly offbeat world views, well … that was a bit much for the inhabitants of the quiet little town.

The twins had been trying to keep low (relatively normal) profiles since the start of summer—largely for he sake of their sitter biz—and tales of ancient curses a mummy run amok would have torpedoed those handily. Likewise, a possessed speaker.

lloooo …" came the sound of the voice again, the nglish accent muffled somewhat—as if it was rson speaking that was lying face down on

possible, and with a flurry of hand odding, Cheryl indicated to Tweed nverse in private, out of earshot of the Drive-In speaker. By the time they'd finished talking, Tweed had shrugged out of the jacket she'd been wearing—even on summer days, her gothy ensembles and milk-pale skin) rarely allowed for bare arms—and as holding it out in front of her like a bullfighter's cape. wly, carefully, the girls crept back to where the speaker on the ground.

"Now!" Cheryl exclaimed. "Get him!"

weed threw the jacket over the speaker and leaped it, wrestling furiously with the—inanimate and actly wrestling back, but never mind—speaker. ed frantically wrapped the material around it, ker squawked like a chicken with a walkie- heryl held out her knapsack and Tweed stuffed sting piece of equipment inside, tugging the shut and effectively muffling its outrage.

3 THE THING FROM (REALLY) BEYOND

The girls ran for the big red barn at the far edge of the Drive-In lot, wherein the headquarters for C+T Enterprises was located. Once inside, with the bolt lock slammed shut on the door, Tweed fished the (inexplicably still yapping) jacket-bundle of what should have been inoperative electronics out of the knapsack and carried it over to the workbench. She set it down hesitantly and took a quick step back.

"Grab a sleeve?" she asked her cousin.

Cheryl reached out and grabbed one cuff as Tweed grabbed the other.

"On the count of three?" Cheryl suggested.

Tweed nodded solemnly.

"One … two … thr—"

"Wait!" Cheryl held up a hand, frowning.

"What?"

"Are we doing one ... two ... *go-on-three?*" she asked. "Or one ... two ... *three-and-then-go?*"

Tweed's brow furrowed to match Cheryl's as she contemplated. It was, in the light of, say, a movie-based action sequence, a matter to be given serious thought. "Good question," she said. "I can see merit in either technique. The first option is probably, statistically speaking, the classic. But I can see how it would leave room for inaccuracy to creep in. The second option establishes the count rhythm more soundly."

"So ..." Cheryl was torn. The jacket sleeve hung limply in her hand. "I say classic?" She didn't sound so sure.

Tweed nodded. "If you think that's bes—"

"Oh, for crying out loud!" the bundled speaker suddenly exclaimed. "Pick one! I'm suffocating here!"

It startled the twins so badly that they both yanked their respective sleeves, the jacket flew up into the air and the defective speaker spun like a top on the workbench. Its red indicator light pulsed in time with the speaker's wails of "WoowOOooWOOOwoooo" as it spun. It looked a little like the light from the top of one of Wiggins Cross's handful of police cruisers on the one and only time the girls had ever seen one speeding down Main Street with light and siren flashing and blaring. That was three years earlier when there had been reports of a stray dog in town.

The twins watched in astonishment as the speaker slowed and stopped, tipping over on its side. There it lay, making strange gurgly sounds.

"Um." Cheryl peered closely at the little piece of equipment. "Sir? Are you ... y'know ... gonna barf?"

"Don't be vulgar," the little metal box responded. "Also ... maybe."

"I can put a bucket out," Tweed suggested, "only, you don't have a mouth."

The red light, which had gone dark as the speaker lay there inert, slowly gleamed to life—almost as if it were a bright red eye opening.

"Harry Houdini's ghost!" the speaker exclaimed.

The girls got the distinct impression that, if it could, it would have skittered backward across the table.

"Where am I?" the thing demanded. "Who are you two urchins? Why do I sound like an old Victrola?"

"An old what-now?" Cheryl asked, agog and still glancing around to see if Pilot or Pops or maybe Artie Bartleby was hiding somewhere, pulling the twins' collective leg.

"A phonograph," the speaker said in answer to her question. "A talking machine."

"You are," said Tweed.

"I'm what?"

"A talking machine." She peered at the speaker from beneath the dark fringe of her bangs, fascinated. The voice was definitely emanating from the defunct speaker. It wasn't a trick—or, if it was, it was the best bit of ventriloquism ever.

"Don't be ridiculous." The speaker sniffed haughtily. "I'm no machine, I'm a magician. I am the Great Simon Omar! Although, I confess that I do feel somewhat strange at the moment ... Fetch me a looking glass."

The girls blinked at each other.

"A mirror, you dim bulbs."

They blinked some more. "Um ..." Cheryl tried to put it delicately as she said, "You ... you don't actually have eyes, though."

"A mirror!" The glowing red light pulsed madly.

"Okay, okay! Don't get your woofers in a knot."

Shaking her head and muttering in disbelief that she was actually taking orders from an inanimate object, Cheryl trotted around to the other side of the workbench. The twins had collected a plastic bin full of mirrors large and small, useful in the vampire-hunting trade for identifying the fiends by their lack of reflection. Cheryl found the bin and rummaged through it, extracting a lady's compact that had a magnifying mirror on one side and a regular one on the other. She passed it over to Tweed who, uncertain as to exactly which bit of the speaker would actually be able to "see" its reflection, held it up toward the front side of the little metal box, where there was a mesh grill through which the sounds of the movie would normally filter. But now, it made the sound of a horrified gasp!

The red indicator light on the top of the speaker blazed alarmingly bright. Tweed and Cheryl found themselves staring at it, and then realized that it wasn't a light at all. Rather, it looked more like some kind of faceted red jewel—like a big fake ruby—that had somehow wound up embedded in the metal housing of the speaker. Apparently, that's exactly what it was.

"The jewel! That's the jewel from my mystic's turban!" the speaker exclaimed as Cheryl poked it with a finger. "Ow!"

"What's it doing in our speaker?" Cheryl asked.

"Well, how should I know? I don't even remember how I got here. Wherever 'here' is ..." The glow from the stone seemed to oscillate, as if it were a crimson eyeball, rolling a glance around its surroundings.

Cheryl and Tweed exchanged a glance.

"What *do* you remember?" Tweed asked.

"Erm ... I'm not sure. I don't know. Why do you ask?"

"How do you know who Dudley is?" Cheryl said in a menacing tone. The whole carnival thing was still something of a sore spot for her, and the mere mention of Winchester P.Q. Dudley's name was generally enough to light her up like a stick of dynamite with a too-short fuse.

The speaker seemed to sense that he'd just set foot, so to speak, on dangerous ground and backpedalled furiously. "Er ... who?" he asked.

"You said his name a few seconds ago."

"Never heard of the colonel."

"Except you know he's a colonel."

"Oops."

"Spill it, Speakie."

"Shutting up now."

Cheryl reached out with both hands as if she was about to grab the speaker by the throat before she realized what she was doing.

"Wait a minute ..." Tweed frowned fiercely, suddenly reminded of something. "Did he say something about a 'mystic's turban' ...?"

"I think so." Cheryl shrugged one shoulder.

"Hang on," Tweed muttered and jogged over to a corner of the barn stacked with an assortment of seemingly random objects the girls had collected from the field across the road after the carnival had so hastily cleared out.

The girls had mostly done their trash collection out of a sense of duty—keeping the field tidy and all, town pride, don't be a litterbug, that sort of thing—but they discovered it was a treasure trove of useful stuff. Things like an enormous Styrofoam mini-donut that must have fallen off the top of one of the food shacks, a jumbo bag of unused industrial-strength glitter and a "You Must Be This Tall to Ride this Ride!" sign.

Who knew when such awesome oddments might come in handy?

Tweed shifted over the height requirement sign so she could get at the contents of a plastic bin they'd filled with the smaller bits of carnival detritus and, after a moment's digging, found what she was looking for: a bunch of note cards from the curiosities tent that had been left behind, scattered amongst the empty display cases (empty because Cheryl and Tweed and Pilot and Artie had loaded most of the assortment of stuff into Pilot's plane so they could send the mummy princess into the Great Beyond, accompanied by her worldly goods). The cards had been printed with paragraphs that described individual items on display and the words *jewel* and *mystic turban* had twigged something in her memory. Tweed shuffled through the little stack of typewritten cards until she found the one she was looking for.

"Aha!" she exclaimed in a triumphantly deadpan monotone. "I thought I remembered something about that …"

"Remembered something about what?" Cheryl asked.

"One of the artifact note cards the carnies left behind had a description on it for something called 'The Spirit Stone of Simon Omar, World-famous Wizard of the West End,'" she said.

"What?" Cheryl blinked. "Who?"

Tweed handed the card over to Cheryl, who held it

up in front of her face and read the faded, typewritten words out loud.

"'Once thought to be a ... uh ... a charl-a-tan and a sham'—"

"Lies!" the speaker blurted.

"Shh!" Cheryl silenced him and kept reading. "'Simon Omar, mystic and stage magician who claimed an ability to commune with spirits in the beyond, shocked and surprised his West End audience during one evening's performance in 1917 when he proved, beyond the shadow of a doubt, that he possessed real magic powers'—"

"Seriously?" Tweed asked, a shadow of skepticism darkening her gaze.

Cheryl shrugged and kept reading. "'The magician's arcane talents were fully demonstrated when he quite unexpectedly'—aw, holy moly, Tweed! listen to this— 'when he quite unexpectedly blew himself to smithereens whilst summoning entities from the beyond!'"

"Right in the middle of my second encore!" the speaker enthused.

"Wow ..." Tweed whistled low. "Way to bring the house down."

"I'll say!" Cheryl peered at the last line of the information card. "Says here that 'the ruby jewel from his gold-lamé turban was all that was left of him' ... Yeesh. Messy."

"Ah yes. I remember now," said the voice wistfully. "That was the performance where I finally managed to punch all the way through to the spirit plane. The afterlife."

"So … what happened?" Cheryl asked.

"It punched back."

The twins flinched in tandem.

"A rather unfortunate incident, really," Simon Omar's disembodied voice continued. "Some departed shades can be a tad on the grumpy side, you see. And if one of 'em decides to throw a spectral temper tantrum, and you happen to make contact at just the wrong moment, they can sometimes muster up an awful lot of arcane energy. The end result is usually nothing more than a dazzling light show and a deafening ka-boom. In *my* case, the entity I'd managed to disturb from eternal slumber decided if I really wanted to talk to the dearly departed *that* badly, then I might as well just … dearly depart."

"Gah!" Cheryl shuddered in horror.

Tweed blinked. "You mean a ghost … *exploded* you?"

"Thereby turning me into a ghost, myself," Simon Omar explained. "And then, it seems, the grumpy old spook trapped that remaining spectral essence in my turban jewel for good measure. Just to teach me a lesson, I suppose. Ah, well … as theatrical demises go, I'm sure it was spectacular! No doubt secured me a place in the annals of famous magicians, wouldn't you say?"

"Um." Cheryl shrugged a shoulder. "We've never heard of you."

"Nonsense."

"No, seriously," Tweed confirmed. "No offence, but you actually kind of wound up bouncing around in the back of a truck, part of a rinky-dink travelling carnival run by a nefarious scammer named Colonel Winchester P.Q. Dudley. Along with a bunch of fake stuff made up to look like rare artifacts. You and the mummy princess were probably the only real curiosities he had. And he probably picked you up at somebody's lawn sale or at a flea market."

"Mummy princess? Dudley?" The speaker actually sounded like it was frowning in thought. "Dudley … ah, yes. It's coming back to me now … flashes of memories of my time with the carnival …"

"What do you remember?"

"Potholes."

"'Scuse me?"

"The carnival truck had terrible suspension," the speaker complained. "I rattled around in my case like a lone pea in a pod! I remember now! And that Dudley fellow. The Colonel. Dreadful showman. No panache!"

Cheryl leaned her elbows on the table, intrigued by the talking speaker. Tweed settled herself on a stool, likewise fascinated. Under normal circumstances, a pair of twelve-year-old girls might not have had such cucumber-cool reactions to a piece of supernaturally possessed machinery. But, then again, Cheryl and Tweed weren't what anyone usually thought of as "normal." And a magic speaker was kind of a step down from the paranormal encounter they'd experienced only a few days earlier (although they'd never suggest such a thing to it—that would be rude).

"D'you remember the carnival's mummy princess?" Cheryl asked. "She's a pal of ours."

"Never met her," Simon answered. "Although, now that you mention it, I do recall admiring her sarcophagus from afar. Never spoke though. I mean, it isn't like I've exactly been the life of the party for the last hundred years or so, y'know. All I could do was lie there like a piece of cheap costume jewellery on that ratty old velvet. That, at least, seems to have changed."

"Well ..." Tweed considered that, her head tilted to one side. "I think it might have been the mystical shockwave blast from opening that portal into the Egyptian afterlife. You remember, Cheryl?"

"Sure." Cheryl nodded. "That explosion lit up the sky like a firecracker going ka-boom!"

"Right! And remember how the portal kinda spat out all of Dudley's carnival junk that didn't belong to the princess?"

"Oh yeah." Cheryl nodded. "It was like a mini meteor shower. There must be Duds—y'know, carnival bits and bobs—all over town! Tweed's right—that must have been what happened to you, Mr. Speakie! That blast shot you through the air with enough force to jam you into that speaker. Well, not you. Your turban-bauble thing."

Tweed peered at the speaker closely. "That was some pretty powerful magic ... maybe it gave you the ability to talk, too."

"Maybe it's just 'cause he's a 'speaker' now!" Cheryl tried not to snort in amusement at her own pun. The speaker sort of glared at her. "Um. Heh. Kinda neat that you managed to keep that funny accent and all ..."

"Now, listen here, missy—"

Suddenly, there was a knocking on the barn door. The twins jumped.

"Hide the squawk box!" Cheryl hissed, shoving the stack of note cards into the front pocket of her knapsack, which was hanging on a hook on the work table, and flapping her hands at Simon Omar. "It's probably Pops!"

"Roger, roger!" Tweed whispered as Cheryl ran for the door.

"Hey!" the speaker protested. "Mfff!"

"Shh!" Tweed said as she grabbed the thing, muffling the sound grill with one hand. "Be quiet now or you'll get us in a heap of trouble!" She stuffed it in a drawer, slamming it shut just as Cheryl pulled back the bolt and a bright flood of sunshine spilled through the doorway, buttering the dusty floor of the shadowy interior like a fresh-popped piece of toast.

It wasn't Pops. It was Pilot.

"Oh, hey there, Flyboy!" Cheryl said brightly, tossing a relieved wave at Pilot as he stepped through the door. "Howzit goin'?"

"Well, my day was going along just fine," Pilot said with a crooked grin, "right up until Pops asked me to check if you girls needed a hand with anything ..."

Cheryl and Tweed noticed then that there was a hopelessly knotted bit of bubblegum-pink skipping rope tangled around Pilot's ankle. In one hand, he carried a beat-up-looking pool noodle, and there was a Nerf dart stuck to the brim of his baseball cap with its suction cup. A light dusting of something that resembled powdered sugar coated one shoulder of his jacket and the side of his face.

Pilot had obviously run afoul of the twins' ACTION!! set-up out in the lot.

"Where in the Sam Heck did you two find a giant Styrofoam mini-donut, might I ask?" he asked, brushing at the fake sugar.

Cheryl grinned and waved in the direction of the empty field across the road from the Drive-In. "Carnival leftovers," she said.

"Ah." Pilot plucked the baseball cap off his head—and the Nerf dart off his cap—and with the sleeve of his jacket wiped his brow, pushing the sweat-damp blond hair back from his face. The day was already growing hot and he wandered over to the big old fridge that sat chugging away in the corner of the barn and fetched himself a cold bottle of soda. "That repair job is thirsty work but I think we've almost licked it. Anyway, Pops wanted me to ask you two if you'd managed to take care of that tweaky speaker. I'm guessing that mess of booby traps out there means you're on the job in your usual no-nonsense fashion." He grinned, knowing full well that the girls never could perform mundane tasks without resorting to a game of ACTION!! "Did you find out which squawk box was wonky?" he asked.

"Yeah! We found it all right!" Cheryl blurted, hardly able to contain her excitement at the girls' new-found mystical phenomenon. A spirit-possessed piece of equipment from right there in their own beloved Drive-In! Pilot would be amazed. "See," she continued breathlessly, "the wires were all frayed and stuff and so we took it down—'cause we figured you could give us a hand later rewiring it, after you're done helping Pops with the second projector—but *that* wasn't what was making it act up!"

"Okay." Pilot shrugged. "I'll bite. What was it?"

"That's just it ..." Tweed took up the tale, serious and ominous. "We were right in the middle of an ACTION!! sequence. But then ... something weird kind of ... happened."

"Weird?" Pilot grinned. "Now why doesn't that surprise me where you two are concerned?"

The girls gave him identical looks.

"Okay, okay." He put up a hand, forestalling outrage. "What weird thing kinda ... happened?"

With a dramatic flourish, Tweed yanked open the drawer and presented the mystically compromised speaker box. "This," she said, gesturing (appropriately enough) like a magician's assistant, "is what happened!"

Cheryl emulated her cousin's flourish (only with a bit more of a jazz hands/ta-da! kind of vibe) and the two of them waited to see how Pilot would react to the talking magic speaker ...

Which suddenly refused to utter a word.

A long silence stretched out in the dusty air of the barn. Pilot scratched at his ear and cocked an eyebrow. The girls exchanged a confused glance and Tweed poked the speaker with a fingertip.

"Uh ... Mr. Omar? Sir?"

More silence.

"Simon?"

No response.

"Who are you talking to, Tee-weed?" Pilot asked.

"The magician," she said, frowning. "He's trapped in the speaker."

"Magician ...?"

"Not the *actual* magician," Cheryl attempted to clarify, adding her own finger-pokes on the speaker's other side. "More like ... his spirit. Mojo. Thing."

The speaker remained utterly inert.

"Hey! Speaker Boy!" she yelled in what would seem most likely to be the speaker's ear. "Wake up!"

Pilot crossed his arms and looked like he was trying really hard not to laugh. Tweed nudged Cheryl with her elbow and gave her a slight head shake. Maybe they'd lost the trans-dimensional connection or something. But one thing was certain: if the not-quite-departed spirit of the magician wasn't going to cooperate, there wasn't much they could do about it.

"Yup," Pilot said, struggling to keep a straight face. "I can see what your problem is. That there is one defunct speaker."

"Oh … never mind." Cheryl glowered at the speaker.

"If you want, I can take it apart and see what the trouble is once Pops and me are done with the projector repairs," Pilot offered good-naturedly as he pulled up a stool to the work table and plunked himself down on it.

"No!" the girls protested in tandem. What if such meddling released the magician's spirit? Or—horrible to think—destroyed it altogether?

"Well, whatever." Pilot shrugged. "Let me know if you change your minds."

Truthfully, Pilot was pretty used to strange behaviour where the twins were concerned, and so their current speaker-based wackiness wasn't all that provoking. He took a long sip from his bottle of soda and put it down on the table, beside a small stack of envelopes and junk flyers. On top of the pile was the strange invitation the girls had received the day before, and the way the sunlight streaming through the barn door shifted in that instant made the embossed gold lettering seem to gleam and pulse with its own light.

"Oh ..." Pilot winced a bit. "I get it."

"Get what?" Tweed asked.

Pilot gestured at the mail. "I see you two got that invitation that was sent out to some of the sitter kids in town."

"Of course we did!" Cheryl said, brandishing the envelope. "It's an invitation to compete for a super-sitter job!"

"Yeah, I know." Pilot raised an eyebrow at the invitation, as if he'd been somehow personally insulted by the little envelope. "And I'm sorry. But, you know. It sounds stupid, and just because you girls can't go is no reason to start acting all crazy. I'm sure there'll be other invitations."

"What?" Cheryl asked. "What are you talking about? Why are you sorry? Why wouldn't we go? This Heck Fellow is looking for the best Wiggins has to offer!"

Pilot looked back and forth between the two girls for a long moment. Then he sighed. "You didn't read the fine print did you?"

"What fine print?" Tweed asked ominously.

Pilot pulled the invitation out of the envelope and pointed to the very bottom. Where there was, in teeny-weeny letters, fine print.

"I thought that was just a decorative squiggle," Tweed muttered, as she reached into a work table drawer and pulled out the magnifying glass the girls had used only the week before to ingeniously pop a kernel of popcorn using only sunlight and patience. Cheryl peered over her shoulder as Tweed hovered the big round glass over the invitation, and together they read the words:

Participants must be 13 years of age or older.

Tweed put the magnifying glass down slowly.

Cheryl stepped back away from the work table. She looked over to where the carnival ride sign stood leaning against the wall. "It's just like that!" She pointed, her lip quivering a bit. "It's like we're not tall enough. We're not old enough? We're the best dang babysitters this town has ever seen. AND we saved the town! This? This is a grave injustice and no mistake about it! I mean, y'know, except for the fact that it's clearly a mistake!"

There was a rebellious gleam in Tweed's grey eyes. "I don't see why we don't just go anyway." Her quiet voice, a counterpoint to Cheryl's more boisterous outrage, was still sharp with emotion.

"Well, why not?" Cheryl jumped right on board that bandwagon. "Why don't we? And prove to this whole town *and* His Lordship Heckenfrankenfurter, or whatever his name is, that we are the best. Thirteen or not thirteen!"

"Whoa, whoa, *whoa!*" Pilot exclaimed, alarmed by the head of steam that was gathering between the two of them. "You girls really haven't thought this through. I mean—for one thing—d'you honestly think Pops is going to let you two out for a whole night in a strange house? He probably wouldn't let you, even if you *were* thirteen!"

The girls exchanged a mutinous glance and Pilot shook his head in exasperation.

"Aw, c'mon!" he said. "It sounds like a whole buncha fuss for nothing. And you don't want to hang out with them anyway—"

"Them?" Cheryl asked pointedly.

"Oh, uh, yeah …" Pilot huffed a heavy sigh and rolled his eyes heavenward, figuring out just how badly Cheryl and Tweed were going to take the news. "I kinda heard Hazel Polizzi talking to Cindy Tyson about the stupid thing this morning. They were hanging out around the ice cream shop when I went to the hardware store to pick up some WD-40 and this new monkey wrench." He plucked the wrench out of the denim loop in his overalls and twirled it on his finger like a gunslinger.

Tweed's gaze narrowed. "What were they saying?"

"That they were going to corner the Wiggins sitter market ..." he said, "baby, pet *and* house—the whole kids and kaboodles!—after they aced the contest."

Tweed ground her teeth and Cheryl snorted in barely suppressed fury.

"They seemed pretty pleased with themselves." Pilot shook his head, an expression of distaste on his face. "Laughing pretty hysterically—joking about all the flyers they'd delivered around town *really* paying off."

"Flyers!?" Cheryl sputtered in outrage. "But ... but ... that's *our* marketing strategy!"

Tweed's gaze smouldered with displeasure and her mouth disappeared into a thin line. "Clearly, our success at the Bottoms Boys' Birthday Bash made an impact on the competition. They've decided to play by the rules in the handbook of dirty tricks."

"No ... girls." Pilot grimaced. "I don't think that's what they meant."

"What *did* they mean?" Cheryl frowned.

"I think they were making fun of *your* flyers."

"Oh."

"I don't know why you girls are so bothered by it." Pilot shook his head. "And I can't believe their mothers would let them go either. So the whole situation is whaddayacallit. Moot."

"Oooh no! There's nothing moot about this!" Cheryl's outrage had her lit up like a firecracker. "Whatever that even means! Unless it means outright war! Then it's super-mooty."

"C'mon, girls. Don't you think there's something just a bit shady about this?" Pilot plucked up the invitation and gave it a narrow-eyed glare.

"Pff." Cheryl waved away his concerns. "Don't be naïve, Flyboy. That invitation is *embossed*. You can't be shady if you're embossing stuff."

"It's true," Tweed agreed. "Shadiness would be indicated only if the invitation was handwritten in red ink that far too closely resembled blood."

"Right! Don't you know anything?" Cheryl crossed her arms over her chest. "Besides, it could be a terrific business opportunity!"

"A high-profile gig like this could really set us up." Tweed nodded. "Think of the publicity."

Pilot shook his head. "I just don't—"

"You can come with us if you're so worried!" Cheryl said.

"No."

"But—"

"But nothing!" Pilot slashed a hand through the air. "I'm *not* coming with you because you're *not* going! Listen. We got off darn lucky last time you two got yourselves in hot water. Imagine what would have happened if Artie had stayed a lizard!"

Tweed rolled an eye. "Crocodile."

"Whatever!" Pilot said, exasperated. "Or if Pops had

found out you two had been driving the Moviemobile around town. Or if my mom had woken up to find me and my plane gone in the middle of the night! We'd all have been grounded until were old and grey!"

A silence descended in the barn in the wake of Pilot's outburst. Clearly he felt pretty strongly about the subject at hand. Cheryl blinked a few times and then nudged Tweed with her elbow. The cousins exchanged a glance and Tweed turned back to Pilot.

"You know something, Pilot?" she said solemnly. "You're right. We don't have anything to prove, do we Cheryl?"

"Uh ... no?" Cheryl tentatively agreed.

"Well, good," Pilot said, picking up his wrench and sliding it back into its pocket loop. "I better go. My mom needs me to do some chores, and so Pops and me are gonna knock off the repairs until later today. It oughta be easier to test out the projector around sundown, anyway. We should have that screen up and running by the time the cars start rolling through the gates tonight, in time to deal with all that overflow from another smash-hit top-notch C+T bill. That's something to take your minds off this house-sitting nonsense, right?"

"Right."

"Sure."

Pilot tipped his hat back, tossed the girls a casual wave and said, "Later 'gators!" Then he was gone.

Cheryl turned and tilted her head at Tweed. "Nothing to prove?"

"One thing to prove."

"And that is?"

"That we're the best dang sitters this town has got!"

4 DIAL S FOR SITTERS

Sundown seemed like a long way away on a summer day as long and sunny and hot as that one. But there was an awful lot to be done if the twins were going to successfully execute OPERATION: DING DONG. First, the girls had to go and tidy the Drive-In lot and pack away all of their ACTION!! gear. Next, they had to gather up all the sitter implements that they thought they might need for a night on the job. In spite of all their claims to expertise, the girls had never before really sat at a house with no actual living, breathing occupants in it, and so they were somewhat unsure as to what tools of the trade they should pack. For instance, the bag of Double Stuf Oreos they usually considered indispensable as incentives—bribes, really—toward good behaviour amongst their toddler charges would be less than useful in a big old empty house that was free of actual children. And besides, the girls would just wind up eating them all themselves.

In spite of what they'd said to Pilot, Cheryl and Tweed knew perfectly well that he was right about one thing. Talk turned to the fact that there was, in all likelihood, no way in the world that their grandfather was about to sign off on them spending a whole night in a strange house. They discussed several ways to get around that particular roadblock.

"Just don't tell him!" Simon the speaker suddenly piped up with the most obvious solution, from inside his drawer.

"Gah!" Cheryl jumped at the sudden crackle of sound. She stalked over to the work table and yanked open the drawer. "Where the blazes were you when Pilot was here?"

"Um."

"You made us look like weirdos, y'know," Tweed said, glaring down at the little metal box. "And that's something we're quite capable of doing all on our own. We don't need your help!"

"Sorry," Simon said. "I'm shy."

"You're a bucket of bolts and wires," Cheryl pointed out. "You can't be shy."

"I was ... napping."

Tweed didn't buy it. "Were not."

"You *told* me to be quiet!"

"And then we *told* you to say something," Cheryl said. "You're kinda lousy at taking direction."

"Look. I'm not sure that I'm ready for the world to know about me," the speaker said. "I mean, except for *you* fine young ladies, of course. What if the constabulary finds out? Or those mad fiends in the scientific institutes? They'll want to take me apart to see what makes me tick! Your friend with the monkey wrench there was going to do that very thing!"

"How come you're talking to us, then?" Tweed asked.

"I like you two. Lots of pluck."

"Whatever." Cheryl rolled her eyes and shut the drawer. "Come on, Tweed."

"Wait!" Simon's muffled voice protested. "Take me with you!"

Tweed wasn't so sure that was a good idea. "Uh ..."

"Why?" Cheryl asked, pulling the work table drawer back open a crack and peering into its dim confines.

"I, well, it's rather embarrassing," the speaker muttered. "After all, I, the Great Simon Omar, have faced the abyss. I have parted the veils between the worlds of the living and the dead. I have summoned forth the ethereal and the terrible, communed with the spirit plane, dazzled and amazed and—"

"And you're afraid of the dark, right?" Tweed asked pointedly.

"Erm ... yes."

Cheryl stifled a snort of amusement. But to be fair,

she didn't much care for sleeping in a room without a night light either.

"Beyond that," Simon continued in a rush, "you're going to need me."

"Need you?" Cheryl asked. "For what?"

"Your house-sitting competition!" he said. "Just think of the kind of advantage a man—er, machine—of my particular qualifications could provide!"

"Well," she mused, "we've already branched out into cat-sitting and, if we manage to book this gig"— she waved the invitation—"house-sitting as well. Speaker-sitting could be just another speciality of C+T Enterprises, I suppose."

"Okay then." Tweed plucked the mystically possessed speaker up out of the drawer and tucked him into the side mesh pocket of Cheryl's knapsack where he could look out and—if it was actually something he needed to do—breathe. "But we're taking you with us on one condition. You have to stay quiet unless we tell you to talk. People in Wiggins already think we're weird enough without us having to explain the likes of you!"

"Deal," the speaker said. "Done."

"Okay." Tweed nodded.

"I'll be hushed as a mouse."

"Good."

"Not a peep out of me. Not one magic word."

"Fine."

"Mum. Dumb. Silent as the grave."

"I get it."

"Dead quiet."

Tweed sighed.

"Not a whisper of a—"

"Zip it, Speakie!" Cheryl finally exclaimed.

Simon Omar crackled with a burst of static in surprise and then lapsed into silence.

"Geesh," she said. "For a speaker, he sure talks a lot."

Tweed knit her brows together in a frown beneath her bangs. "Are we *seriously* not going to tell Pops about this?" she asked.

"If we do, there won't be any 'this.' He won't let us go."

"It's not fair. Hazel and Cindy are almost the same age as us. And they didn't just save the town from a supernatural incursion. We did that."

"Sure." Cheryl shrugged. "*You* know that and *I* know that and, well, *that's* kind of the problem. It's not like we can tell anyone. Aside from Artie and Pilot, that intel stays classified. Eyes Only. Not only would no one believe us, but they'd think we were funny-farm material. Even more than they already do."

"Pops would believe us," Tweed muttered.

Pops, they'd always known, *didn't* think the girls were crazy.

"Maybe ..."

"He'd believe us and then he'd ground us."

"Yup." Cheryl felt the sudden rush of a blooming rebellious streak. "But it's not like this is going to be the same thing. It's just a big ol' pile of non-paranormal bricks. No kids and no craziness, right? And it's not as if we haven't already proven ourselves in the arena of super-sitting! We can totally handle ourselves."

"Sure we can."

"Sure you can!"

"Gah!" Cheryl almost jumped out of her skin yet again. She nudged the speaker in her knapsack sharply with her elbow. "Shh!"

"I told you! I can be useful. Let me prove it."

"How?"

"I've got an idea. A way you two can convince your granddad to let you off the leash for the night."

"What can I do for you, Cheryl?" Pops asked, tipping the baseball cap off his head and wiping the sweat from his brow. Tufts of white hair sprouted like dandelion fluff on either side of his head above his ears. He walked over to the refrigerator in the sunny farmhouse kitchen and fetched the big glass pitcher of lemonade that was always kept full on hot summer days and poured himself a glass.

He gulped thirstily as Cheryl took a deep breath and crossed her fingers behind her back.

"Well," she said, "um, me and Tweed wanted to know if you'd be okay with us spending the night at … um … a friend's place." She winced involuntarily at the fib and hoped Pops wouldn't notice. "For a sleepover."

Pops tugged his hat back onto his head and frowned faintly. "Tonight?"

Cheryl nodded.

Pops scratched at his ear. "That's awfully short notice, don't you think?"

"Um … well … yes," Cheryl stammered, casting about for just the right words to convince Pops of the benefits of such an outing to his two beloved granddaughters. "But it's a once-in-a-lifetime opportunity!"

"Oh? Why's that?"

"Well, uh, it's with Hazel Polizzi," Cheryl said, not *exactly* hedging the truth—after all, according to Pilot, their sitter nemesis (and their other sitter nemesis)—had already jumped at the chance to partake in the Hecklestone invite. "And Cindy Tyson'll be there, too."

"Aren't those young ladies babysitters here in Wiggins, too?" he asked.

"Exactly!"

Pops's frown turned to a look of confusion. "I thought you didn't get along so good with them."

"Oh, heh, that! …" Cheryl laughed a bit too

loudly but Pops didn't seem to notice. "Water under the bridge! Heh! Buried the old hatchet, we did! Very thirteen-years-old for a couple of twelve-year-olds, don'tcha think?"

"Well, I must say, I'm very proud of you girls."

"Thought we'd, uh, celebrate with a, um, professional retreat of sorts. A sleepover sympodium."

"I think you mean sym*pos*ium."

"Right! A sitter summit! A meeting of the minders, so to speak." She was babbling and she knew it, but she couldn't help herself. If Pops didn't let them go, then the greatest business opportunity of their young entrepreneurial lives would just slip right through their fingers. "Heh. You know, us girls will trade advice: movie suggestions to soothe rambunctious charges, share some bedtime tips, toddler-tantrum tricks, tooth-brushing techniques … er … Popsicle etiquette …"

She trailed off finally into silence as Pops stood there contemplating. Finally, he took a last gulp of lemonade and set the glass down on the counter. Then he nodded decisively.

"I think that's a wonderful idea," he said. "The Polizzi place, you say?"

Cheryl stayed silent, neither confirming nor denying Pops's assumption of location—which was quite fortuitously located on the other side of Wiggins and so not a place Pops could just amble on over to in order to check out the truth of the tale.

"I don't know the Polizzis very well ..." Pops mused, rubbing his chin, his gaze drifting over to the telephone hanging on the kitchen wall. "Maybe I should just give them a ring, see if there's anything I can send over for the party—"

"Capital idea! I'll dial!" Cheryl exclaimed, relieved that Pops wouldn't actually pay the Polizzi abode an in-person visit. She fairly leaped across the room and, standing between Pops and the phone, dialed a number. When it started to ring on the other end, she stretched out the cord and handed over the receiver, holding her breath.

"Hello?" The voice was muffled by the press of Pops's ear but Cheryl could still make out the slightly nasal tones saying, "Polizzi residence. Mr. Polizzi, proud father of Hazel and loving husband to—er—Missus Polizzi, definitely speaking."

Pops blinked for a moment, then held his hand over the mouthpiece and whispered to Cheryl, "Sounds like an English fella. I thought the Polizzis were Italian."

"Isn't Italy pretty close to England?" Cheryl asked with an innocent shrug. "They're both on the other side of the ocean ..."

Pops returned the shrug and uncovered the phone. "Why, hello there, Mr. Polizzi," he said jovially. "My name is Jefferson Pendleton—most Wiggins folk call me Pops—and I don't know that we've ever been rightly introduced, but I run the Starlight Paradise Drive-In theatre here in town. I understand you and your missus are very kindly hosting a slumber shindig for some of the Wiggins girls tonight?"

"Right you are, my good gentleman purveyor of celluloid entertainments!" said the voice.

Pops blinked at the phone. "Uh … right. Well, I was wondering if there was anything you'd like me to send along with the girls?"

"Popcorn and jujubes! Maybe some of those cellopacks of licorice ropes! Milk Duds! Also … one moment please … ah, right! Might come in handy if you can send along any glow tape, road flares, bicycle pumps and any old spare rapiers you might have lying around for the purposes of duelling. Ow! What?" There was a pause, punctuated by garbled whisper-mutters, then the voice came back on the line. "Sorry, old chap! The little woman gets a bit gabby at times—ow! Stop poking!— you know how it is … Well, gotta toddle! We'll have your girls back to you all in one piece come sun-up— heh heh, I hope! Ow!"

5 HARRIED AT THE HOUSE!

"**H**uh." Cheryl swung her leg over the seat of her trusty ten-speed bike as she dismounted. "This is it, I guess ..."

"Y'know," Tweed said, braking into a dramatic gravel-throwing side slide, "I never noticed this big ol' iron gate here."

"Yeah ... me neither."

"Not surprising, I guess, considering that we never actually noticed a whole darn road here ..."

"Well, Wiggins Cross *is* an awfully big place ..." Cheryl giggled at her own expansive sarcasm.

Tweed cracked a smile at the joke and hefted her knapsack higher up on her shoulders. Pops had miraculously said yes to the sleepover and even supplied the girls with provisions—granola bars instead of Drive-In Snak Shak goodies—but, sadly, he'd drawn the line at rapiers and flares. Cheryl hefted her pack, too, made heavier by the weight of one (so far quiet and well-behaved) Drive-In speaker.

"44678," Tweed said, brushing the overgrown ivy from the numbers on the gate. "That's the right address."

"Funny that. I mean, far as I can see, this house is the only house on the street. You'd think they'd just number it 1."

"Enh. Rich people are weird. Let's go."

The gate creaked like the lifting of a coffin lid in one of the girls' monster movies. Which probably would have sent chills up their spines if they weren't so darned used to the sound. All that was missing, really, was the sound of an organ playing a hollow, haunting strain as they walked their ten-speeds up the overgrown path toward the stone manor. All along the path, in nooks carved into a cedar hedge, classical-style marble statues stood frozen in elegant poses, their once-gleaming white surfaces faded with neglect and tinged green in places with mossy growth. On the leaf-strewn path, a pair of garden lizards ambled along, oblivious to the twins' presence. And at the end of the path stood the imposing edifice of the house of Hector Hecklestone. The darkened window arches above the massive double door seemed to glare down at the girls like the empty eye sockets of a skull, and the creepy silhouettes of winged gargoyles perched on the roof peaks.

The girls tucked their bikes in behind a tall wall of cedar hedge, grown shaggy and in need of pruning to the extent that it looked as though it might actually come to life—some kind of terrible green monster that might devour the girls' bikes while they were inside. A rusted rake and an abandoned pair of hedge trimmers added to the effect. It looked as if the house's last hapless gardener had, perchance, fallen victim to the leafy monster, mid-trim.

A chill breeze raised the small hairs on the back of the twins' necks.

Yes. A chill breeze. That was it.

"Right." Tweed cleared her throat. "So."

Cheryl glanced around uneasily. "Think Cindy and Hazel are here yet?"

"I don't see their bikes ..."

"Maybe the hedge ate them."

"Heh. Heh ..."

A spooky silence descended, broken only by the sound of the hedge rustling in the aforementioned chill breeze. Neither of the girls so much as took a step forward toward the house.

"Hey," Tweed said, eventually. "Why don't we work up a quick game of ACTION!! to get us into our groove?"

"Capital idea." Cheryl nodded vigorously, gesturing

at the overgrown hedge. "Swamp monster scenario? Jungle epic? Mutant plant-life invasion?"

"I have a better idea," Tweed said with a grin.

"You do?"

She pointed first at the marble statues, then at the gargoyles on the house and the pair of garden geckos. "We've never really done a classic stop-motion-style sequence before, have we?"

Cheryl returned her cousin's grin, instantly seeing where she was going with this. One of the staples of the B-movie genre was, of course, the time-honoured art of stop-motion special effects. Epic battles fought between brave warriors and enchanted stone monsters—or mythic warriors or skeletons brought to life or impossible winged creatures—were shot using tiny models that were photographed frame by frame and then combined in a sequence with live actors. Such scenes were often combined with giant-creature smackdowns where the filmmakers used to dress up iguanas or turtles in pointy, scaled hats or glue spikes to their shells and shoot them in extreme close-up on papier-mâché sets to make them look like enormous prehistoric dinosaurs or mutant monstrosities instead of run-of-the-mill garden critters.

Jason and the Argonauts, the Sinbad movies and the original *Clash of the Titans* all employed the glories of the lost art of stop-motion. And the front yard of the Hecklestone House seemed as if it would benefit from some likewise fanciful action. Really liven up the old place. And with the appropriate props already in place, all it needed was ...

Cheryl cracked her knuckles. "Cameras rolling ..."

Tweed flipped her hair back over her shoulders. "Aaaaand ..."

"... ACTION!!"

EXT. ANCIENT ISLAND TEMPLE -- DUSK

CAMERA PANS DOWN from a HIGH OVERHEAD SHOT
of a TINY ISLAND in an AZURE SEA, ZOOMING
IN on the ELEGANT COLUMNS, OLIVE TREES and
CLASSICAL STATUES that dot the crest of the
ISLAND's ONLY HILL.

                                    CUT TO:
A PAIR OF ADVENTURER-WARRIORS, dressed in
TUNICS and SANDALS and CRESTED HELMETS,
carrying SWORDS and SHIELDS. They leave their
ship and approach the silent steps leading up
to a MOSAIC TERRACE fronting the temple.

                WARRIOR TEE
            (in a tense whisper)
    We must be careful. This island was
    cursed by a powerful sorceress. None
    who have ventured here have lived to
    reveal its secrets ...

                WARRIOR CEE
            (in a confident whisper)
    That's because they were them and not
    us.

                WARRIOR TEE
    Good point. We're the only us there
    is.

                WARRIOR CEE
    That we are.

As they pass a STATUE of ARES the WARRIOR
GOD, the vacant marble eyes GLOW TO LIFE and
FOLLOW THEIR MOVEMENTS!

                                        CUT TO:

CLOSE-UP on the WARRIORS: They are
ferociously fearsome.

The WARRIORS step forward confidently, ready
to face any challenge. Except, maybe, *this*
one.

CAMERA PANS suddenly back toward the STATUE,
which has COME TO LIFE!! WITH A SOUND LIKE AN
AVALANCHE, ARES's FEET break loose from the
statue's marble base!

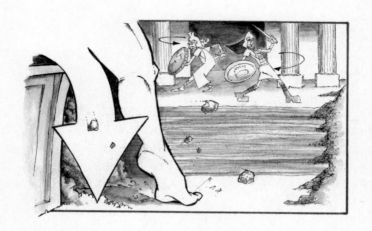

The ground trembles as he strides forward,
swinging his GREAT STONE SWORD!!

                    WARRIOR TEE
          Great Zeus!

She LEAPS out of the way, as the sword
whistles over her head!! The two do BATTLE!

                    WARRIOR CEE
                      (shouting)
          Leaping lizards!

                    WARRIOR TEE
              (over her shoulder as she fights)
          Hey! You're quoting Little Orphan
          Annie! Wrong movie!

                    WARRIOR CEE
          No! I meant -- LEAPING LIZARDS!

She points to where a pair of GIANT-SIZED
DINOSAUR-LIKE CREATURES AWKWARDLY LURCH
TOWARD THEM. The creatures HISS and SCREECH.
They BRISTLE with GIANT SPIKY SCALES. The
WARRIORS are cut off from the TEMPLE.

The reptiles lumber in pursuit ... but are
distracted by the sudden appearance of a
GIANT VENOMOUS TOAD!!

The monsters FIGHT!

The WARRIORS dodge between them.

WARRIOR TEE dive-rolls over the spiky,
swishing tail of one of the reptiles.

WARRIOR CEE ducks and runs straight
through -- BETWEEN THE FRONT LEGS OF ONE OF
THE CREATURES!

They *almost* reach the temple steps ...
Suddenly, WARRIOR TEE points to the skies
with her sword!

                    WARRIOR TEE
     Look! Doom from above!!

                    WARRIOR CEE
     Doom from above ... meet death from
     below!

WARRIOR TEE blinks at her companion.

                    WARRIOR TEE
     Ooh. Nice quip. I say we run for it.

OVERHEAD CAMERA shot frames the WARRIORS as
the SHADOWS OF GIANT BAT-WINGED CREATURES
SWEEP OVER THEM. They bound up the TEMPLE
steps ...

Right into the STICKY TRAP OF A GIANT
SPIDERWEB, STRUNG FROM PILLAR TO PILLAR.

                    WARRIORS CEE + TEE
     EEEEeeeewwww ...

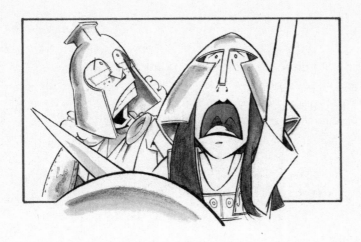

They untangle themselves. WARRIOR TEE is
paler than usual. WARRIOR CEE is all fired
up. Her eyes narrow and she points her sword
at something over WARRIOR TEE's shoulder.

                    WARRIOR CEE
          Ah. The "piece of resistance." The
          climactic Giant Tarantula battle.

CAMERA CLOSE-UP ON: WARRIOR TEE's eyes --
saucer-wide beneath the brim of her helmet.

                    WARRIOR TEE
          Climactic ... Giant ... What ...?

CAMERA WIDENS OUT to show a GIANT HAIRY
SPIDER LEG, POISED TO TAP WARRIOR TEE on the
SHOULDER.

                    WARRIOR TEE
      Cut. CUT. CUTCUTCUTCUUUUUUTTT!!!

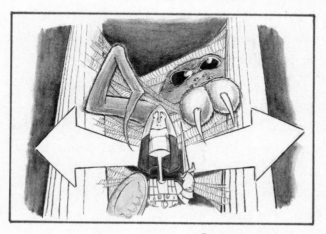

"CUT!! ..."

Cheryl gaped at her cousin, as Tweed gyrated across the porch in a dance of sheer, flappy panic, screeching "CUT!! CUUUTTT!! Yikes! Cut!"

"Whoa! Tweed!" Cheryl lunged for her and grabbed her by the shoulders before she toppled off the porch and into the shrubbery. "TWEED! While-O-Wait, partner! While-O-Wait!"

Tweed froze, compelled by the power of the W-O-W chant. Her hands were clenched into fists in front of her, and her eyes were squinched tight. "Get it off!" she squeaked. "Getitoff getitoff getitoff ... GET IT OFF!"

"Er ... okay ..." Cheryl assumed she meant the itty-bitty spider that was sideways-creeping across the top of her head, and so she reached up and gently plucked the wee thing from Tweed's dark hair and carried it over to the porch railing, shooing the bug from her palm with a breath of air. "Scoot," she said and waited until the spider had scuttled out of sight. Then she turned back to her cousin, trying her best not to stare in shocked surprise at Tweed's monumental freak-out.

"Is it gone?" Tweed asked, cracking open one eye.

"It's gone."

She opened the other eye and a blush of embarrassment crept up to displace the normal pallor of her cheeks.

"So." Cheryl cleared her throat. "Spiders?"

"It's true. I'm arachnophobic."

"I just thought you were afraid of spiders."

"That's what that means."

"Oh. Right. I just—"

"I looked it up." Tweed kicked at the surface of the porch with the toe of her black, many-buckled boot. "It's embarrassing. I'm supposed to treasure the macabre, revel in the creepy, delight in the freaky-outy. You know. Things exactly like, well, spiders."

Cheryl shook her head, somewhat astonished that she'd never known this about her cousin. The girls had always just taken it for granted that they knew everything about each other. But as close as they were—as close as if they were actually twins with each other—they didn't.

"I never would have guessed," she said.

Tweed winced. "You won't tell anyone, will you?"

"Heck, no."

"If this got out to the general populosity, it would totally destroy my spooky street cred."

Cheryl put a hand on Tweed's shoulder, casually removing a second little bitty spider that was harmlessly perched there, without drawing Tweed's attention to what she was doing. "Your secret's safe with me, pal. Nice to know we can still surprise each other," she said, nonchalantly depositing the bug on a branch out of Tweed's line of sight.

"Thanks, pal."

6 OPERATION: DING DONG

"**O**kay, then," Tweed said as she squared her shoulders and turned to face the door of the house. "Enough excitement. Ring that bell!"

"Right!" Cheryl turned to the door of the house and raised a hand, one finger extended. Then she paused and looked around. "Huh."

"What is it?" Tweed asked. "Not another spider?"

"Oh no, nothing like that." Her gaze swept the frame surrounding the door. "Just that ... there's no doorbell."

"Huh." Tweed peered closely, confirming the absence of buzzer or bell.

Cheryl frowned. "Does this mean we have to change the mission name?"

"I say keep it." Tweed shrugged. "I like 'Operation:

Ding Dong.' We'll just say it's ironic. Besides, 'Operation: Knockers' might give people the wrong idea."

"Right." Cheryl nodded. "Okay. So … what do we do now?"

For some reason, both the girls were still feeling somewhat reluctant, even after their bout of ACTION!! Now that they were really there, standing on the threshold of the old manor house, Cheryl glanced nervously at the sky. She knew that her imagination was a pure and potent force to be reckoned with, but even she had been surprised by how real their ACTION!! game had felt. Especially when the winged shadows had swept over them. She'd actually thought she'd felt a chill.

But that wasn't the real reason for her reluctance.

"What if ol' Heckenwhozits sends us away?" she asked. "I mean, we are kinda crashing this party. The invite specifically said—"

"I know what it said!" Tweed said, rather more snappishly than she intended. She took a breath. "Sorry. I mean, I know what it says, but we're here to convince him we're up for the job, right? And we are, right? We can do this?"

Cheryl had never really heard her cousin sound unsure of herself before. The spider encounter must have shaken her up more than she would admit. "Of course we are," Cheryl said firmly. "And of course we can."

She gave Tweed the C+T Secret Signal (patent

pending). Tweed grinned, some of the usual grimly gleeful sparkle returning to her eyes. She gave Cheryl the Signal back, turned toward the door, lifted her fist … and lowered it again.

"Knock," she said to Cheryl.

"You knock," Cheryl said back.

Tweed's mouth disappeared in a thin line. "Okay, Fine. I'll … um …"

"Just get on with it already!" Simon Omar's voice startled them both.

Frankly, both girls had quite forgotten he was there.

"You're killing me with all this suspense!" he continued. "No, wait … I'm bored. So bored. You're boring *holes* in me!"

Cheryl reached into the mesh side pocket of her knapsack and brought the speaker up to her face. "Now listen here, Speaker Boy, we'll run this mission how we see fit. We don't need some exploded old-timey Ouija-board substitute giving us orders."

The speaker started making noises that sounded distinctly like a chicken clucking. Cheryl and Tweed exchanged a glance. Maybe having spent all those years trapped in a gaudy bauble and unable to communicate had damaged the ex-magician's sanity.

"Bo-ock … bock-bock-bock-bock …"

Or maybe Simon Omar was just calling them chicken.

"Hey!" Cheryl exclaimed upon the realization.

Tweed grabbed the speaker from Cheryl and held it out toward the enormous, heavy-looking oak front door. It looked like something transplanted from a medieval castle. It had heavy bronze hinges on one side and a large, ornate bronze doorknob right in the middle of the carved wooden surface. It was strange ... the hinges were dull with tarnish, but the doorknob seemed almost to glow, as if it had been recently polished.

"You wanna get this show on the road so bad?" she said, glowering her best gothy glower. "*You* knock!"

"No knuckles," the speaker pointed out.

Tweed ground her teeth together audibly and went to shove the speaker back in the bag.

"Wait!" Simon exclaimed. "All right, all right. I'll put my lack of money where my lack of mouth is. Go ahead—bash me on the door, why don't you, and ... uh ... now, hang on just a minute ..." The red glow from his "eye" stone swept the door from side to side and stopped, focusing into a narrow beam, aimed at the big bronze doorknob. "Hey! I know that knob—"

Suddenly, the door swung open, and the twins jumped a foot in the air. Cheryl hastily grabbed Simon back from Tweed, stuffed the squawking speaker into the main pocket of the knapsack and yanked the drawstring tight, silencing the wacky mystic's protests. It wouldn't do to show up unannounced at the Hecklestone manor both underaged—according to the snooty invite—and lugging along a mouthy disembodied magician in a metal box. That was sure to make them unwelcome.

The girls peered into the yawning maw of the house but all they could see, beyond the glow from the porch light that lit up only a few feet of Persian carpet, was shadow-shrouded darkness.

"Um ... hello?" Cheryl called out. She cleared her throat to try and rid her voice of a wobbly quaver. "Mr. Hecker—"

"Hecklestone," Tweed hissed.

"Right. Mr. Frecklestone?"

Tweed sighed.

"Anybody home?"

The door creaked as it swung open another few feet. It sure seemed like an invitation to go on in and make themselves at home ... or something to that effect. So they did. That was what they were there for. The girls squared their shoulders and lifted their chins and stepped over the threshold, wearing their widest, brightest best-dang-sitter smiles.

Cheryl held their business cards out while Tweed had a neatly folded three-colour flyer to present, but as they stepped into the soaring, elegant, opulent ... also dim, dusty, spooky ... foyer, there was no one to give them to.

"Uh ... Mr. H?" Cheryl glanced around. She even checked behind the door. The place echoed with her voice.

"Maybe he's got the door on remote control," Tweed suggested.

"I would have expected at least a butler in an upscale hoity-toity joint like this." Cheryl crossed her arms.

"Kinda been left without the Lurch here it would seem," Tweed joked, riffing on that spooky old *Addams Family* TV show. "Heh. Maybe this is one of the so-called challenges mentioned on the invitation."

"What kind of a challenge is this?" Cheryl snorted. "How to break-and-enter without the 'break' part? I mean—we just, y'know, entered."

A breeze slithered down the grand curved staircase and sent little whirlwind eddies of dust dancing across the black-and-white-tiled floor. From somewhere far away, they heard the flapping of wings—birds in the attic, maybe, or bats—and the girls unconsciously assumed a defensive back-to-back stance. It was disconcerting to feel as if they were being watched in a house that seemed, at the same time, to be so completely empty.

Cheryl gulped. "Tweed?"

"Yeah?" Tweed felt a shiver run up her cousin's spine that seemed to transfer over to her own and she clutched her elbows tightly.

"Maybe ... I dunno. I'm starting to think that maybe this wasn't one of our better ideas."

"I'm starting to think you're right," Tweed agreed.

"Let's go back outside and wait on the porch and see if anyone else shows up—"

SLAM!! went the front door.

"Or …" Tweed suggested in a dry whisper, "maybe we could just run home right now and never come here again!"

"Good plan!"

The girls ran for the door, but before they could get to it, the big bronze doorknob—gleaming with a sullen, greenish light in the gloom—made a sound like someone was turning a key in its empty keyhole. There was a loud, echoing *ker-chunk,* like a door to a prison cell locking up tight, and when the girls tried to turn the knob, it refused to budge in either direction.

Wild-eyed, Cheryl ran for the window beside the door. It was tall and heavily curtained. When she pulled the drapes aside, she discovered it was locked and painted shut. It wouldn't budge. The glass was sturdy-looking, thick and rippled in places. Cheryl wondered whether she could throw the foyer's tall wooden coat stand through it.

Tweed, for her part, seemed to have recovered a measure of her usual calm self. Or maybe she was just scared stiff. Cheryl couldn't quite tell. "Nobody knows we're here, do they?" she asked.

"Nope," Tweed answered.

"We probably should have told Pops," Cheryl said quietly.

"Then he wouldn't have let us come and we wouldn't be here."

"Exactly."

Tweed turned in a tight circle. "Maybe we should have at least told Pilot."

"Then he would have told Pops and he wouldn't have let us come and we wouldn't be here."

"Exactly." Tweed hugged her elbows and frowned. "I feel like a sneaky jerk. We never should have lied to Pops."

"Nope. And so do I." Cheryl let the curtain drop. "But we've made our bed and now we're gonna have to sit on it."

"I guess so."

After a moment, Cheryl tried to lighten the sombre mood a bit. "You know who we should have told?" she said.

"Who?" Tweed wondered.

"We should have told Artie Bartleby."

"What?" Tweed quirked an eyebrow at her cousin. "Why? He wouldn't have told Pops. He would have bugged us to tag along and we would have let him, and then we'd still be right where we are, except he'd be here with us and annoying the heck out of the both of us."

"Yup."

"Yeah." Tweed smiled grimly. "You're right. It would at least have given us something to take our minds off the extremely high creep factor going on here ..."

"Plus, he was actually pretty useful during the whole cursed mummy episode."

"I kinda miss the scales and teeth he had when he went all possessed-reptile-minion ..."

"Don't forget the tail!"

The girls started to relax, remembering just what a sight Artie had been on that crazy carnival night, with his glasses perched at a wonky angle on his crocodilian snout and a mouthful of snaggleteeth that gave him one heck of a drooly speech impediment. But even mystically monsterized by a cursed mummy princess, Artie had proven himself remarkably resourceful. Reminiscing about it in that moment actually gave Cheryl and Tweed a nice shot of encouragement.

"Listen," Cheryl said, "if Shrimpcake could handle that, then we can handle this. And you know what? Maybe this is just another one of those challenges the invite mentioned. You know, see how well we react under stress and all that."

"If it is, we probably just bombed out on that one," Tweed murmured, stepping farther into the gloom of the old house. "Wonder if Cindy and Hazel will be able to handle it better than us ..."

"Pff." Cheryl was reasonably certain that there would be no contest on that front. After all, Cindy was most likely still sporting bite marks from her last less-than-successful sitter gig over at the Bottomses' family house. And there was a rumour widely circulating that Hazel still hadn't gotten over the time that little Binky Barker had taken a hammer to her cellphone. "I'm not worried about those two. And our brief hiccup will soon be forgotten as we demonstrate our mad sittin' skills, partner."

"Do you think any of the other Wiggins sitters accepted the invite?"

"Maybe. I guess we'll find out soon enough …"

"Right." Tweed yanked her jacket straight and squared her shoulders. "So. Mission objective?"

"I'd say recon first." Cheryl nodded decisively. "Check the place out. Get the lay of the land."

"Check."

Tweed gave Cheryl a bonus C+T Secret Signal (patent pending) and off they went. It was easier to push aside their initial apprehensions once they got focused on the reason for being there in the first place. No doubt the lack of host to greet them was all part of the test to see how they would handle themselves. Not throwing a coat stand through the front window in an immediate escape attempt was sure to score them points right off the bat. Confidence and competence were the order of the day.

First, they checked out the dining room to the left of the foyer. There was a long dining table set with twelve chairs on each side and one tall armchair at the head of the table. Tall silver candelabras stood in the middle, set with unlit candles.

"Okaaay," Cheryl said after a quick circuit. "Moving right along …"

Back through the foyer and over to the other side, a set of tall double doors stood open, leading to a combination living room/study. On one wall was an enormous stone fireplace, logs stacked in the grate, with an assortment of heavy mahogany and leather furniture facing it. The air in the house felt weirdly heavy—as if the girls were walking under water. Dust motes hung in the air, swirling like swarms of tiny insects as Cheryl and Tweed moved through the room.

"Boy," Cheryl said, "this place could use an update. Lighten up the decor a little, you know?"

"Yeah." Tweed nodded. "Even I have to admit that the whole early-Munsters vibe is kind of a downer. I mean, creepy chandeliers, grandfather clocks, suits of armour ... it's all a bit obvious."

"Agreed." Cheryl shoved her hands into the pockets of her jeans and rocked back and forth on her sneakered feet. Then she strode briskly back out into the grand marble foyer. "Ho-hum. This is pretty typical fare as far as creepy old manor houses go, wouldn't you say, Tweed?"

"Oh definitely. No surprises here," Tweed agreed, striding equally briskly beside her cousin. "Except, of course, for that piano teetering precariously at the top of the staircase ..."

"Oh ..." Cheryl's sneakers squeaked to a halt on the marble tile as she stopped and looked up to see a majestic, shiny black piano slowly rolling forward over the lip of the top step of the great sweeping staircase, like a ship in full sail cresting a wave. "Yeah ..." she said. "That's not something you see ... every ... uh-oh."

With a roar like an onrushing locomotive, accompanied by the sound of its own silent-movie off-key tinkly piano, the shiny black grand piano suddenly tipped forward and thundered down the stairs. Eight hundred pounds of crushing musical mayhem headed straight for Cheryl and Tweed, who froze on the spot, transfixed by the spectacle.

"LOOK OUT!" Cheryl shouted.

She dove left and Tweed dove right. Thank goodness for all that rigorous physical training the girls put themselves through to keep their sitter skills keenly honed. Also, Cheryl's stunt-double aspirations were really starting to pay off. Whereas, only a month or two earlier, she might have escaped rumbling-piano death by a hair's breadth, on this particular occasion, she escaped rumbling-piano death by a hair's breadth—*and* looked good doing it! Her forward dive transitioned smoothly into a classic shoulder roll and when, at the end, she popped back up into a bent-kneed fighting stance, it was with little effort and only a mild wobble. An 8.5 out of 9.

Of course, no one was there to applaud her or post a score, other than Tweed, who, Cheryl was glad to see, had avoided being crushed in her own inimitable style. Her dive had carried her into the far corner by the cobweb-festooned coat stand, which she'd grabbed on to and used to spin herself around so that she could launch into a ninja-esque flying kick that neatly dispatched the piano bench thump-thump-thumping down the stairs after the grand piano. As Tweed's kick sent the bench careening harmlessly down the hallway, Cheryl was already halfway up the curving stairs, flailing fists stirring the dusty air before her as she sought out the source of the piano pushing.

There was no one.

By the time Tweed joined her at the top of the stairs, Cheryl had thoroughly inspected the empty landing and had found it, well ... empty. The girls looked over the railing, down through the mushrooming dust cloud at the mess of kindling and keys and discordantly twanging wire that had once been a lovely old Steinway.

"Guess there will be no encore tonight," Simon muttered from Cheryl's knapsack pocket.

"Shh!" Cheryl shushed him.

Tweed's gaze narrowed beneath the fringe of her straight dark hair. "Who the heck called that tune in the first place?" she wondered.

"What the heck kinda test was that anyway?" Cheryl glowered. "Agility? Musical appreciation?"

"I *really* didn't appreciate that," Tweed said grimly.

Cheryl frowned. The long, wide hall branched off in three directions, but all of the corridors were empty. The tall doors set into the corridor walls at regular intervals were all closed, except for three, which stood wide open. Cautiously, the twins approached the first door and saw that there was an ornate brass nameplate in the middle of it.

"'Daphne,'" Cheryl read.

Tweed moved on to the next one. "I've got 'Edwina' over here," she said.

"This one says 'Roderick,'" Cheryl noted of the third open door. "So Heck's got kids, I guess."

She poked her head into the room to see a neatly made boy's bed in the middle of a chaotic mess of old-timey rocket ship models—all brass rivets and gears and cogs—and all sorts of unidentifiable bits of machines in various stages of disassembly. In one corner, a Junior Professor–style laboratory table was set up, and there was a faintly sharp tang of rotten-egg smell hanging in the air.

Edwina's room was full of dolls, sitting on the canopied bed, tucked into carriages, perched in tiny high chairs or riding doll-sized rocking horses—all of them draped in lace handkerchiefs, as if they were dressed as ghosts for Halloween.

In Daphne's room, the walls were covered with picture frames. Which was, the girls supposed, fairly normal. Except for the fact that every single one of them was turned around to face the wall.

"Huh. Weird …"

Cheryl reached out and turned the nearest frame around. It housed a black-and-white photographic portrait of a family—mom and dad and three kids: a boy and two girls who looked to range in age from about seven to ten.

"Hecklestone family ancestors?" Cheryl said.

"Guess so," Tweed agreed. "I gotta say, I'm not surprised Daphne has the pictures turned around if they all look like this. Who wants to go to bed every night with that bunch of sourpusses glaring at you?"

She had a point. The expressions on the faces of the portrait subjects were uniformly unsmiling. Mom and Pop looked resigned, stern and a bit bored. But the three kids stared into the camera with the kind of intensity the girls could almost feel. Their eyes seemed to glitter darkly. Cheryl shivered and turned the photo back to face the wall.

"Old pictures really creep me out," she said. "Except, y'know, old pictures of the 'moving' variety."

Tweed nodded in total agreement.

A sudden whispering, hissing noise sounded like it was coming from the hall. The girls turned back to see that another door was now open directly across the way. They exchanged a shrug and crossed the hall to find a large dressing room. The room was dark, but they could see, from the illumination cast by the glowing wall sconces out in the hall and the last blue gleam of dusk filtering through tall windows, that it was stocked with expensive-looking clothing—for both boys and girls—

hanging from rows of hangers or tucked neatly into cubbyholes and dressers.

"Boy, the Hecklestone kids have got a pretty sweet set-up here, don'tcha think?" Cheryl said.

She looked over to see Tweed inspecting the black lace trim on a particularly gothic-looking gown and Cheryl could tell that she was moments away from drooling or trying it on.

"Oh, yeah." Tweed sighed longingly.

"Well, I guess once Mr. H gets the family settled in Wiggins, they'll probably get homeschooled or shipped overseas to some kinda schmancy boarding school ..."

Cheryl wandered a few steps farther into the dressing room.

Over along one wall stood three identical full-length mirrors, ornately framed and tall enough to double as doors. In the twilight gloom, she could see that, marring the polished surface of each looking glass—at varying heights and of varying, but all rather smallish, sizes—there was a handprint.

"Guess it's the maid's day off," she said dryly, and reached out with the hem of her shirt to wipe away one of the prints.

Only ... it seemed as if the handprint was on the *inside* of the mirror. She scrubbed at it, but it remained indelible. Cheryl pushed her glasses up her nose and peered closely at the smudge ...

WHAM!!

"What the—?!" Cheryl jumped back, startled, as a hand, fitting the size of the print, suddenly slammed up against the mirror! Or so it seemed ... Cheryl blinked and rubbed at her eyes and looked again. There was nothing there. She ran to the other mirror and thought she could see a figure, wide-eyed and open-mouthed, pressed up against the other side of the glass. "Who the—?!" In the third mirror, she thought she saw the flash of shiny black shoes running past. "Where the—?!"

"What's wrong?" Tweed called from over by the rack of sumptuous dresses.

"Hit the lights!" Cheryl called and heard Tweed instantly scramble around, looking for a wall switch or pull chain. When she found it, there was a loud CLICK and the ornate overhead fixture glowed to orangey-yellow life.

"What is it?" Tweed asked, rushing over to see what had startled her cousin.

Cheryl peered closely at the mirror. And then the one beside it. And then the one beside that. Nothing. Not even the handprints she thought she'd seen. "Uh ... nothing ..." She shook her head. "I guess."

A gloomy silence shrouded the house. And then ...

Giggling.

"D'you—"

"Shh!" Tweed silenced her cousin and pushed her hair back from her ear, cocking her head and listening.

In answer to Cheryl's unasked question, yes—she clearly heard it, too. The sound of mocking laughter, echoing and distorted, drifted through the house. But the owners of those voices were nowhere to be seen.

The girls stepped out into the corridor and tiptoed back to the main hallway, where the three corridors branched off.

After a moment …

"That way!" Cheryl whispered, pointing down one of the corridors. The girls took off at a silent run. Tweed took the doors on the left side and Cheryl took the ones on the right. There seemed to be dozens of them— almost as if the corridor was growing longer the farther down it they went—but eventually they reached the end. After much turning and jiggling of knobs and peering through darkened keyholes, all the girls learned was that they were all locked. They shared a perplexed moment at the end of the hall and then turned to retrace their steps … only to see that all the doors—every single one of them—now stood wide open.

"What the …?" Cheryl blinked and did a double take.

"Interesting," Tweed said.

"I'd bet our hourly sitter rate—snacks included— that Cindy Tyson and Hazel Polizzi are behind this." Cheryl glowered at the shadows painting the hallway in stripes of gloom.

"You think?" Tweed was skeptical. "Isn't trying to

crush us with a piano going just a little overboard? Even for those two?"

"You know, they're probably freaking out because we totally *owned* that Bottoms Boys' Birthday Bash gig," Cheryl said. "We left them with a lotta cake on their faces. I'm pretty sure they're not going to forgive us for that any time soon ..."

"Yeah, but ... a *piano*?"

"Harsh, I know. But what else could it be? Maybe they just meant to push it to the top of the stairs and lost control. But I think they're trying to rattle us out with these 'spooky' shenanigans." Cheryl put air quotes around the word *spooky*, just in case Cindy and Hazel were around somewhere, spying on them and operating under the false impression that she and Tweed were the least bit rattled. Because they weren't. At all. Not one bit. No siree—

SLAM!!

The door nearest them slammed shut with a resounding *crack* like a thunderclap and the girls nearly leaped out of their skins and took off down the corridor to the main hall! As they ran, the doors on either side swung closed one after the other—SLAM!!SLAM!!SLAM!!SLAM!!SLAM!!—all the way along. Except for the very last door. Even after they'd made it past, back to the landing at the top of the stairs, it still stood widely ... *weirdly* ... open.

7 A ROOM WITH A BOO!

Cheryl and Tweed exchanged a glance and, communicating through their exclusive series of custom hand signals, agreed to investigate. They backtracked toward the door—crouching low and using the tall dusty vases and hall tables spaced along the walls as cover—and approached with extreme caution. First Tweed poked her head around the door frame, then Cheryl did.

"Okaaay ..." Tweed said.

"All riiight ..." Cheryl glanced around.

"There's, um, nothing here."

"Nope. Nada."

"Okay, so ... what's the deal? Why is this door open? This room's mostly empty."

It was indeed. Furnishings in the room were

sparse—a large oak desk stood at the far end of the room facing a marble fireplace, paired with a wingback leather swivel chair. Nearby stood a small round table, draped in a cloth and surrounded by simple wooden chairs. An elaborate crystal chandelier hung from the middle of the ceiling, right above a wide open space that looked as though it should have been furnished, but wasn't. One wall was occupied by tall French doors draped in long white curtains that stirred slightly in a breeze coming from … somewhere. Floor-to-ceiling bookshelves lined the other walls, but the bookshelves were empty. Not so much as a dime-store paperback rested on them.

The girls stepped over the threshold into the room, eyes sweeping the corners as if there was definitely something—or someone—hiding there, in plain sight.

"Maybe this was the room the piano came from," Tweed suggested, waving at the empty expanse.

Cheryl shrugged and took a step farther into the room. When nothing leaped out to attack her, she took another one. Her footsteps were muffled by the thickly woven area rug that resembled a giant chessboard, and only the creak of the floorboards beneath indicated her movement.

"Cool rug," she murmured, balancing on one foot on a black space, her eyes crossing as she stared at the alternating black and white squares.

"Rug? What rug?" Simon the speaker's voice came

from the depths of Cheryl's knapsack, loud and crackling and frantic. "Wait! Stop! Both of you. I know you told me to be quiet but you have to trust me on this one—*don't* take another step!"

The twins froze—not really because Simon had instructed them to do so, but more because he'd startled them half out of their wits. Still balancing precariously on one foot (she was afraid to put the other one back on the floor after such a dire warning), Cheryl shrugged out of one knapsack strap and reached around into the bag. She pulled the speaker out and frowned at it. The red Spirit Stone was pulsing like a warning alarm.

"Turn me around so I can see the rug."

"Um, okay ... Er, turn you which way now?" Cheryl fumbled a bit with the speaker.

"Point me at the floor," Simon said in an exasperated tone. "My turban stone. Point the jewel in the direction I need to look."

Cheryl did as she was told, with a silent Tweed looking on in fascination. The red gleam of the Spirit Stone swept the rug beneath Cheryl's feet like the beam from a crimson-bulbed searchlight. After a few moments, it stopped and seemed to narrow its focus on a spot on the far side of the room. "Aha!"

"Aha?" Tweed asked.

"I knew it. It's an old stage magician's trick."

"What is?"

"The pattern of the rug is designed to confuse

the eye," Simon said. "And camouflage the trap door beneath."

"Holy moly! Trap door?" Cheryl handed the speaker over to Tweed, who kept it trained on the corner of the room, and pulled out her trusty mini-golf putter—she'd had the thing for so long the rubber grip had shredded to pieces and fallen off, but she couldn't bear to part with the hole-in-one guarantee—and tapped the rug in front of her.

"Careful …" Tweed cautioned as Cheryl paced slowly forward. "Careful …"

Beneath the rug, the floor seemed solid enough … until she got to the spot where Simon Omar's crimson light shone brightest. Then there was a hollow-sounding *THUNK*. Cheryl dropped down onto her hands and knees and crawled slowly forward, sweeping the palms of her hands over the surface of the carpet as she went.

And … there it was! A seam in the carpet, hidden by the pattern, just as Simon said it would be. She worked the ends of her fingernails under the close-fitting fibres and peeled back the edge of a square of the rug. A square that covered a hinged wooden door. The slightest pressure on the surface of the trap and the thing collapsed inward. It snapped back into place, completely invisible to the naked eye, after a few seconds.

Tweed gasped. "Anyone unlucky enough to step on that square of floor would drop into who *knows* what kind of fiendish trap!"

"A tiger cage!" Simon suggested with gruesome enthusiasm. "Or a dungeon! Or a pit lined with sharpened stakes! Or—"

"Or maybe it's just a plain old laundry chute," Cheryl said.

"Well, where's the fun in that?" the speaker grumbled.

Cheryl snorted. "Since when are dungeons fun?"

Tweed spun Simon around so that she was looking him in the face. Sort of. "If you're really a *real* magician," she asked suspiciously, "then how come you know all about cheap tricks like trap doors and stuff?"

"What? Oh. Um. Well, uh, yes," the departed mystic stammered. "My competition, you see! Uh ... *they* were the ones resorting to chicanery and sleight of hand."

"While *you* were the one performing real feats of supernatural derring-do, huh?" Tweed raised an eyebrow.

"Exactly!"

"And your final act?" Cheryl said, stepping carefully around the trap door and rejoining her cousin on the other side of the room. "The 'mystical ka-boom'?"

"That's right! That's what it was. An ectoplasmic conflagration born of a catastrophic mystical convergence."

"Not, say, too much black powder in a flash pot?" Cheryl suggested.

"What do you take me for?" Simon protested haughtily. "A charlatan?"

It was a bit disconcerting the way the speaker almost seemed to exhibit facial expressions. Tweed handed it back to Cheryl and wandered over to the empty bookshelves next to the door. They were coated with a thick layer of dust, but there were also bare patches where rows of books had clearly stood. Recently. She peered closely and discovered a smattering of fingerprints in the dust, too. Made by small hands. She was about to call Cheryl's attention to them when suddenly, the leather desk chair at the far end of the room creaked.

Cheryl and Tweed froze.

In the silence that descended on the room, they could hear a thin, thready whisper of sound. Like faraway music. As quietly as she could, Tweed stuffed Simon in her knapsack so that she could have both hands free in case emergency hand-to-hand combat was required. Then together, she and Cheryl crept silently toward the other end of the room. The chair was one of those expensive, richly upholstered numbers with the high backs—a perfect perch for an evil villain to spin around on and reveal himself as the mastermind of some nefarious plot ...

Well. The twins had seen enough movies to know that you didn't want a guy like that to get the upper hand. So, instead of waiting for some kind of dramatic reveal, they crept stealthily up behind the chair, ready to give it a good hearty spin. Once in position, Cheryl held up her hand and did a silent three-count with her fingers.

"One ... two ... thr—"

"Wait!" Tweed mouthed, grey eyes wide.

"*What?*" Cheryl mouthed back.

"Are we doing one ... two ... *go-on-three?*" Tweed asked in a sub-whisper. "Or one ... two ... *three-and-then-go?*"

The age-old dilemma.

Cheryl frowned. "*Uh ...*"

Too late! The chair suddenly spun around.

"GAH!!" the girls yelped in tandem and leaped back as the ominous hidden figure revealed himself to be ... a fellow babysitter. Wearing headphones—the source of the ghostly music the girls had heard—and playing a video game on a tiny handheld screen.

"Hey, guys!" Karl Wu peeled off his shiny red headphones and bounced up out of the impressive leather chair. "What's shakin'? You two got that crazy invite, too, huh?"

"Er ... yeah," Cheryl said, composing herself after the near heart failure and glancing sideways at Tweed. "Yeah, we did."

"And we're *totally* allowed to be here," Tweed said, returning Cheryl's glance.

"Awesome!" he said. "I thought I was the only one here in this stupid old house and, lemme tell you, the boredom was kicking in big time!"

Karl "Feedback" Wu was known around Wiggins Cross as something of a techno-wizard (and aspiring lead guitarist for an as-yet-unformed but soon-to-be-wildly-popular rock band). He was the same age as Pilot—

fourteen—but Feedback sported the kind of perpetually cheery grin and bouncy, wound-up, go-get-'em attitude that made it seem like he was actually a lot younger than that.

The twins didn't know him all that well, but what they did know of him, they liked. The only thing that tweaked their suspicions was his—in their opinion—over-reliance on technology. The fact that he could walk, talk, text and play cartoon zombie-smasher games on his newfangled phone all at the same time made them wary. The twins, of course, relied on oldfangled technology that was far more trustworthy. Anything with a computer chip in it was, in their eyes, instantly suspect. And probably prone to government (or possibly alien) tracking.

"Hey! I saw your flyers," he said. "Nice work. Do you guys have a website?"

"Uh …" The twins exchanged another set of nervous glances.

"Tweed doesn't like spiders," Cheryl blurted.

"You promised not to tell!" Tweed hissed.

Cheryl grimaced. "Sorry. Bit frazzled here …"

But Feedback didn't seem to notice the exchange. "Y'know," he said, jumping out of the chair and wandering into the middle of the room without taking his eyes off the phone in his hand, "I've never sat for a place that didn't have any kids in it before. It's kinda weird. And I haven't found a refrigerator yet. Or a kitchen for that matter. And these hallways go on for miles! I thought I was stuck in a maze or something. Feels like I've been wandering up and down the same darn corridor for an hour now. Also? I think this place has maintenance issues. And rats. I keep hearing noises in the walls."

Neither of the twins could get a word in edgewise, but for the moment, that was okay. They needed to gather all the necessary intel they could before they shared their own conclusions about the direness of the situation.

"Have you guys seen Hazel or Cindy yet?" Feedback continued. "I texted them yesterday and they said they were gonna be here, too. Maybe they chickened out. Have you found a TV? Or a sound system? Or a video game set-up? Man, I could *totally* go for pizza pops ..."

"What are you doing?" Cheryl asked finally, pointing to the phone.

"Oh. Looking for a signal." His sunny demeanour clouded over with a sudden, deeply perplexed frown. "I've been trying to pick something up ever since I got here and I don't get it. I'm not getting *any*thing. Like—capital N nothing. No signal—hey wait! 'No Signal.' That's a great name for a band!" He paused and made a note on his phone and then continued. "I mean, Wiggins Cross has super-crappy wi-fi at the best of times but I customized this baby so that I could pick up a signal from the moon! Only ... this house is, like, a totally *dead* zone."

"Yeah ..." Tweed nodded grimly. "That's kind of what we're afraid of."

A sudden crackling of frost spread across the window next to them as the temperature in the room instantly plummeted.

"Whoa," Feedback said, and the girls could see his breath. "Old Mr. H better get the heating/cooling system serviced in this dump. That a/c is turned up way too high ..."

There was another crackling sound—only this time it came from overhead—and Cheryl dove for Feedback, shouldering him out of the way just as the room's overhead chandelier came crashing down in a perilously musical, rainbow-coloured explosion of brass and crystal.

Feedback gulped and whispered, "Thanks ..."

In the silence that followed, they heard the sound of laughter, high-pitched and echoing. Feedback blinked and looked up at the hole in the ceiling where the light fixture used to hang.

"So ... *not* rats?" he asked.

Tweed shook her head and bent to examine one of the crystals.

Feedback knit his brow in an angry frown. "Wow. Maybe Cindy and Hazel did show after all! I mean, I knew those other babysitting girls were hard-core, but that's a pretty lousy way to try and win a stupid contest. They coulda busted open my melon with a stunt like that!"

"Yeah …" Cheryl tugged her pigtails straight, a frown creasing the freckles on her nose. "That's what I thought when the grand piano came crashing down the stairs at us, but …"

"I'm not so sure," Tweed murmured, staring up into the hole in the ceiling.

"Oh, c'mon." Feedback snorted, looking back and forth between the twins. "What—you guys think this place is, like, *haunted* or something? That there's, like, what … supernatural creatures skulking around?"

Suddenly, the French doors flew wide open and the long white curtains billowed like ghosts of departed opera divas making grand entrances. A frantic flapping outside in the twilight gloom sent Cheryl and Tweed scrambling for cover. Tweed dove behind the wingback chair while Cheryl dropped to all fours and scuttled under the desk, dragging an astonished Feedback with her.

"Das Wampyre!" Tweed whispered.

"Das what?" Feedback yelped.

"Shh!" Cheryl hissed.

A winged shadow swept into the room. Sure enough, it looked as if it was being cast by a giant bat right out of an old Dracula movie. The twins held their breath. Mummies bearing curses and possessed inanimate objects were one thing. Ghosts … well, that was something else. But honestly. Vampires? *Real* vampires? They were another thing entirely!

Cheryl tracked the shadow's progress as it flowed

across the wall … dipped awkwardly … and then did a kind of flailing loop-de-loop thing and dropped like a stone. A loud crash sounded from the other side of the room, over by the table and chairs, but she couldn't see what had happened.

A clumsy Creature of the Night? she wondered. *I suppose it's possible …*

"Well, that's just spiffy," Cheryl muttered under her breath.

Whatever the thing was, it certainly wasn't graceful. Still, something had to be done. Not having anticipated any kind of scenario that included fangs, the twins had gone light on vamp prep when they'd packed their respective gear bags for the night at Hecklestone House. They were only equipped with a pair of emergency stakes (really, just a couple of broken school rulers) and a jumbo plastic shaker bottle of dried garlic flakes. Not nearly as effective on Creatures of the Night, perhaps, as whole fresh bulbs, but then Tweed had recently used chili powder to deflect a mummy attack. Anything that could potentially cause sneezing was a useful addition to a weapons inventory.

Tweed could hear Cheryl muttering and digging around in her bag and knew she was probably searching for their emergency stakes. If only Tweed could manage to prepare a garlic Nerf grenade in time, it might give Cheryl the chance to find the weapons and then they both might be able to get the heck out of there. Tweed fumbled in her bag as quietly as she could for kitchen spice and a sponge ball, and readied herself for attack. If she could draw the deadly attention of the fiend, she could give Cheryl the needed precious seconds to launch a secondary attack from behind.

Vampire fighting was all timing and strategy.

And it was a darn good thing that the twins had been honing both those skills for most of their young lives. At a strangled gasp from Feedback, Cheryl glanced up from her pack to see a person-shaped shadow slithering up the wall. Feedback's eyes grew huge as a pair of shiny, pointy-toed black shoes, visible beneath black trouser legs, walked slowly, ominously across the chessboard rug. They stopped directly in front of where Cheryl and Feedback crouched beneath the desk. Feedback held his breath, and Cheryl gripped her ruler so hard the edge of it bit into her palm.

Then a pale face, mostly obscured by darkness, popped down to peer at them.

"Good eeEEee-ven-ing," a voice intoned in a classic Dracula drawl. "Allow me to intro—GLAA—"

The vampy greeting was cut short as, with a furious battle cry, Cheryl launched herself at the creature's knees, bowling him over and knocking him out into the middle of the room.

"Kill it!" Feedback screeched in terror.

"Stake it!" Tweed shouted, frantically readying a garlic bomb.

"Darn it!" the villainous vampire exclaimed as the black silk cape flipped up over his face, effectively tangling the evil creature in a helpless heap and rendering his struggles largely ineffectual.

"Got it!" Cheryl cried triumphantly, raising the ruler over her head.

"Mff! Mff!" the vamp protested, muffled by the bundle of cape cloth. "MFF-GLAACK!!"

"Wait!"

Tweed suddenly leaped into the fray, flinging her cousin off the thrashing creature of darkness before Cheryl managed to pin him to the carpet with her stake. Cheryl tumbled into a series of shoulder rolls initiated by Tweed's dragging, and popped up onto her feet, in a fight-ready, fists-flailing stance.

"What didja do that for?" She frowned at her cousin in confusion.

"That 'GLAACK!!'" Tweed explained, pointing at the writhing heap of evening attire on the floor. "I *know* that 'GLAACK!!'"

"What?" Cheryl blinked at her. "You don't think ..." She turned and nudged the bundle on the floor with the toe of her sneaker. "Artie Bartleby?"

"Mrff ..."

"What on *earth* are you doing here?"

Artie sprang to his feet, threw back the cape he wore draped over his shoulders and ran a hand over the top of his head, smoothing down chunks of rogue hair spiking out in random directions. Beneath the cloak—which, they now saw, looked more like a swanky private school formal robe—he wore a tailored suit jacket, emblazoned with a crest of some kind, and a pressed white shirt and striped black-and-red cravat tied neatly at his throat. Giving them a super-suave wink, accompanied by an enhanced finger point, he grinned.

Tweed and Cheryl were both rendered utterly speechless.

8 PANICKED ROOM

Tweed was the first to recover. "Uh … *Artie?*" Her jaw drifted open at the sight of their former annoying mini-nemesis turned stalwart sidekick/handy fall guy. There was simply no earthly way that the Artie Bartleby the twins knew and (occasionally) loved to tease mercilessly could pull off *that* level of sophistication. No. Way.

"Ladies," Artie Bartleby said, sauntering casually over to the fireplace where he leaned on an elbow and struck a debonair pose. The suit he wore was so meticulously tailored and pressed you could have sliced cheese on his trouser creases.

The twins exchanged uncertain glances and Cheryl took a cautious step forward. "What's the deal, Shrimpcake?" she asked, eyes narrowing as she took in his drastically altered appearance, head to shiny-shod foot. "You a creature of evil again? All minioned up? Possessed? Cursed? What's the deal?"

"Don't be foolish, my little cauliflower," he said and laughed a devil-may-care laugh. "I'm my same old, same old self."

"Uh-huh …"

He licked the tip of his baby finger and ran it along the quirked contour of his eyebrow, above his horn-rimmed glasses—which somehow suddenly looked chic when paired with the tailored duds. "Clothes make the man, don'tcha know?" Artie said, and grinned.

At that point, Feedback crawled out from under the desk. He brushed some carpet lint off his cargo pants and straightened the headphones circling his neck.

"Hey, hey, Feedback!" Artie said with a smooth wave. Helping out at Bartleby's Gas & Gulp, his mom's gas station and general store, meant that Artie knew pretty much everyone in the town of Wiggins Cross.

"That's my name, don't wear it out!" Feedback offered Artie a wobbly grin and air-guitared a riff on his phone that ended with a screech of crunchy amplifier feedback.

The distorted noise bloomed out, echoing loudly in the high-ceilinged room, and there was an answering screech from over near the French doors. A blur of flappy, growling movement surged toward them and Cheryl suddenly remembered the winged shadow that had preceded Artie into the room and lent him the illusion of vampirosity.

The thing flew at Feedback, who dropped to the floor and covered his head. Grey, bat-like wings slapped at the air, obscuring glimpses of red gleaming eyes, a sharp-hooked beak and talons—all attached to something the size of a large house cat!

"Ramshackle!" Artie yelled. "Down, boy! Girl! Thing!"

Tweed looked at him in astonishment.

"I haven't really had a chance to figure that out yet, okay?"

"Shrimpcake!" Cheryl was trying to shoo the whirlwind-scrabbling creature away from poor Feedback, who cowered in a ball. "What on earth is that thing?"

"I found him out on the balcony!" Artie said. "He's harmless! C'mere, buddy ..." He darted forward and grappled with the hissing, spitting mini-monster, pulling it away by the scruff of its neck. "Sit!" he said, admonishing him with a pointing finger.

The thing cocked its head and regarded him sideways.

"Siiiitt," he said again.

"Grr-mrowf," Ramshackle murmured and, after a moment, sat.

"Whoa ..." Karl said in almost a whisper. "What the heck *is* that?"

"Uh ... house cat?" Artie tried unconvincingly, seeming to have just realized that maybe Feedback wasn't as used to weirdness as Cheryl and Tweed. "Exotic breed.

Millionaires, y'know." He waved vaguely at the opulent architecture all around them.

"Artie"—Tweed took a step forward, peering at the little monster—"is that a *gargoyle*?"

"Well, I dunno." Artie shrugged. "I think it's probably a safe bet, though. He was perched on the roof of this creepy old house when I found him."

"Mrrr-ackk-k-rrowr...?" the gargoyle burbled inquiringly and ruffled his batwings.

"Wait." Cheryl frowned, sifting through hours and hours of monster movie flotsam that had settled in her brain. "Aren't there legends that tell of stone carvings—household guardians—that come to life after sundown?"

"You got that from an old Saturday morning cartoon show!" Feedback protested.

"Well, where do you think *they* got the idea from?" she shot back.

"Right. Okay. Y'know what?" Feedback said, trying to be casual, but edging along the wall toward the open door that led out into the corridor. "This was fun. But I'ma gedoutta here..."

Ramshackle issued what sounded like a warning growl, deep in his throat.

"Oh, relax, Feedback." Tweed rolled her eyes and slipped her knapsack off her shoulders. She fished out a bag of Fancy Beast Seafood Deelite Kitty Treats she had stashed in there for (sort of) just such an occasion. When the girls had expanded their sitter services to include pets, they'd stocked up and always carried a bag or two in their supplies, just in case.

"So …" She raised an eyebrow at Artie. "Ramshackle, huh?"

She tossed a fish snack toward the beast and he leaped for it, snapping it out of mid-air with his sharp beak. But one batwing flapped awkwardly, and a clumsy attempt at a barrel roll ended with him cartwheel-crashing to land in a heap. The little monster lurched to his feet and shook his head, with an expression on his face like a cat who, having done something dumb, adopts an "I meant to do that" kind of air. He licked his beak and purred, "Rrr-yumm."

Artie shrugged. "Kind of fits, right?"

They could see that the membrane that stretched between two of the critter's wing points was ragged along the edge.

"He's got a bum wing," Artie said. "I think he musta been hit by lightning or something when he was stone and it chipped his flipper."

"Poor little guy," Cheryl said, kneeling down so Ramshackle could amble over and sniff at her outstretched hand.

"Poor little guy?!" Feedback sputtered. "He's a monster! And … and … impossible and stuff! You all know that, right? I mean—how is … *that* … even possible?"

"Well …" Tweed tried to phrase her answer carefully

so that Feedback wouldn't freak out any more than he already had. She exchanged a glance with Cheryl, who nodded for her to continue. After all, they were, it seemed, in this together. And withholding vital information from Feedback wasn't fair. "Remember when you said you thought Cindy and Hazel might be pranking us on all this stuff and we said—"

"This house is *not* haunted!" he protested before Tweed could even bring up the idea. "There's no such thing!"

"Well, see ..." Cheryl grimaced. "That's what I said, too. But *that's* the trap. In every haunted house movie ever made, someone always says, 'That's impossible! There's no such thing!' which, of course, is always the dead giveaway that it *is* possible and there *is* such a thing."

"But ..."

"We've fallen for the oldest horror movie trope on celluloid." Tweed sighed. "We're Freddy and Marlene on a trip up into the attic during a power failure."

"You're who?" Feedback blinked in confusion.

"We are indeed, partner." Cheryl nodded sagely. "Oh, the irony."

"*Seriously.*" Feedback turned to Artie. "What are they talking about?"

"Beats me." Artie shrugged. "But whatever it is, they're probably right. I say go limp, roll with it, do whatever they say. With luck, the scales and fangs disappear in time for dinner. Or, maybe, bedtime!"

"I … I don't even …"

"If our working theory is correct and this is, in fact, a haunted house, then that"—Tweed pointed to Ramshackle—"being one of the gargoyles from the roof of the house, is equally haunted. Or, at least, animated by some kind of residual essence of the structure."

"Okay. That's it." Feedback began his doorway-bound edging along the wall again. "Like I said, it's been fun, but I'ma *really* gedoutta here!"

"MMRroowr-rrgg …" Ramshackle suddenly sprang to his feet, growling and hissing, staring at the empty air just to the left of where Feedback was slowly making a break for it.

SLAM!!

The door slammed shut and the sound of a key turning in a lock echoed loudly in the wake of the noise. Feedback lurched for the door handle but it wouldn't budge. He put an eye to the keyhole and hollered for Cindy and Hazel to cut it the heck out and open the darn door! When that didn't work, he ran through the French doors and out onto the balcony. The twins could see him peering into the darkness below. After a few minutes of pacing and peering, he came back in, a defeated slump to his shoulders.

"We're really high up," he said. "And there's a killer thorn hedge all the way along under the balcony. We're stuck."

"Yup." Artie nodded sagely. "In a definitely haunted house."

An ominous rumble of thunder sounded in the distance outside and a freshening breeze blew the curtains and rattled the windows.

"Haunted." Feedback shivered. "That's heavy. I mean … I've never even had a measly déjà vu, let alone a full-on paranormal experience."

"No problemo." Cheryl clapped him on the shoulder. "We'll talk you through it as we go."

"You guys sound like this kind of thing happens to you all the time."

"Recently?" Tweed shrugged.

Cheryl nodded. "Yeah. It's kind of a long story. Speaking of which, why *are* you dressed up like that, Shrimpcake? And how'd you get in here?"

"I got into the house in the first place down one of the chimneys," Artie explained.

"You what?"

"Yeah. All the outside doors and windows were locked up tight, but we figured if you guys had found a way in here, so could we."

"Who's 'we'?" Cheryl asked.

"Me an' Armbruster."

"Pilot's here?!" the twins exclaimed in tandem.

"Oh, sure," Artie said. "We shimmied up a drainpipe, straight up the side of the house to an old widow's walk on the roof, and then Pilot lowered me down through a chimney flue with a rope. I landed in a big old pile of soot and was black from head to toe, so I popped into the first bathroom I could find and had a quick bath."

"You had a bath in a strange house?" Cheryl asked.

"Well, it's not like I used bubbles or nothin'," he protested.

Tweed rolled her eyes. "Well, I guess that makes it perfectly normal, then."

"Right?" Artie looked to Feedback for support. "Only ... when I got out of the tub, all my clothes were gone. Shoes, everything. I locked that door—I swear I did. But suddenly it was wide open and there I was, with not a stitch to preserve my modesty except these snappy duds I found hanging in the closet in the adjoining room. Pretty swell threads, huh?"

"So what were you doing out on that balcony then?" Tweed wondered.

"I went out to signal up to Pilot that I was in and stuff, but I couldn't see him," Artie said. "And then I got stuck out there when the doors closed shut and locked behind me!"

Cheryl walked over to the hall door and jiggled the handle. Still locked. "Am I the only one who feels like we're babysitting for a buncha spooky little brats who like to play games?" she asked.

Before anyone could answer, they were startled by noises that sounded like they were coming from inside the wall. Cheryl ran back and picked up her trusty putter from where she'd left it over by the trap door and hefted it like a club. Tweed crouched over her knapsack and emptied it out to find her Nerf crossbow. Together, the twins took up defensive postures in front of the empty bookcase that seemed to be the source of the sound. Artie motioned for Feedback to take cover and assumed his best approximation of a karate stance.

Silence fell on the room.

Then came a sound like a lever tripping. The bookcase wall suddenly shifted and moved, sliding to the side, and a cold shaft of moonlight illuminated a figure standing on a hidden spiral staircase.

A figure wearing a baseball cap and a wry facial expression.

"Well," Pilot said, "at least you didn't lie about hanging out with other sitters tonight ... you just lied about where."

9 SPEAKER OF THE HOUSE

"We didn't lie!" Cheryl protested. "We just ... er ... took creative licence with ... um ... a few key details."

Pilot just shook his head at her.

"Hey, Yeager!" Feedback bounced forward, grinning widely with relief. "Am I ever glad to see you!"

"Hey, Karl," Pilot returned the greeting. "Howzit going?"

"Well, y'know ... interesting ..."

"Yeah. It usually is where these two are concerned." Pilot glanced pointedly at the twins.

"Hey, Armbruster!" Artie stepped forward, hands on hips. "How'd you get inside? I don't see you covered in a chimney's worth of soot!"

"Nope." Pilot brushed at his sleeve. "Just splinters and sawdust. After I lowered you down, the roof where I was standing gave way and I wound up crashing into the attic. That's where I found the top end of this staircase." He hooked his thumb over his shoulder at the wrought-iron spiral hidden behind the bookcase.

"How'd you guys even know we were here in the first place?" Tweed asked.

"I went back to the Drive-In around dusk to help Pops finish up with the projector repairs, and he mentioned that you two were off to a 'sleepover sitter seminar' with Hazel and Cindy. And seeing as how I happen to know just how likely *that* scenario is, I figured you'd done exactly what you said you wouldn't do … and so I came here to talk some sense into the two of you before you got yourselves in any real trouble!" Pilot descended a few more steps and paused. "Of course, first I had to stop off at the Gas & Gulp to get a map because I never even heard of an Eerie Lane in Wiggins. That's where I ran into Artie, and I figured I might need a bit of backup if you two were already in some kind of a fix. Which I somehow suspected you might be when we got here and found your bikes by the gate but all the doors and windows locked up tight!"

Cheryl stuck out her chin mutinously. "We can totally handle ourselves just fine, Flyboy."

Tweed squared her shoulders. "That's right. This situation is *totally* under control."

Pilot blinked at them and then tilted the brim of his cap back. "Oh," he said. "Well, okay. I guess we'll just totally leave you to it then. C'mon, Art-Bart—"

"Wait!!" the twins cried out as Pilot started partway back up the spiral stairs.

Pilot stopped and turned, waiting.

"Um," Cheryl murmured reluctantly. "Maybe you guys should hang around for a bit. Um. Y'know. You don't want to miss out on the ... er ... fun?"

"If by 'fun,' you mean getting the heck outta this creepy old pile of bricks, I'm all for it!" Pilot yanked his cap back down on his forehead and descended the stairs. "Well, c'mon, then," he said, heading toward the door to the hall. "Let's get—"

"NOOO!!" Cheryl, Tweed, Artie and Feedback all lunged forward as Pilot stepped off the last stair and into the library, and the bookcase slid closed behind him. Pilot spun back around but he wasn't fast enough. They could see no mechanism for opening the door on that side of the bookcase.

"I guess we probably should have mentioned that, along with totally being able to handle ourselves ... we're also totally trapped in this room," Tweed said dryly.

"Right." Pilot gritted his teeth. "Yeah ... that might've been useful to know."

He walked over to the door and tried the handle. Then he walked out onto the balcony and looked down. Then he looked up. Then he walked back into the room, sat down in the leather chair Feedback had recently vacated, turned his hat around backward like he always did when he needed to concentrate and sighed deeply. The pilot's wings pinned to his hat glinted in the moonlight coming in through the window.

When Ramshackle, seeming to sense that the newcomer to the situation needed a bit of consoling, came out from where he was crouched in the shadows under the desk and rubbed against Pilot's leg, Pilot absent-mindedly reached down to give what he thought was a house cat a head skritch.

The others watched him silently for a moment.

Cheryl bit her lip to keep from giggle-snorting as Pilot's fingers registered the presence of stubby little horns on the 'kitty.' His hand froze. His eyes went wide.

Ramshackle made an enquiring "Mrrr?" and ruffled his wings.

"WHOA!!" Pilot leaped from the chair and backed into the middle of the room.

"He likes you!" Artie grinned.

"Is that …?"

"A gargoyle?" Cheryl finished Pilot's question for him. "Yeah. You might just wanna roll with this one, Flyboy."

"MRrrwff?" Ramshackle tilted his head.

"He says he likes your wings," Artie said. When Ramshackle issued forth another little burble of noise, he turned to him and nodded. "Yup, he flies, too. Just like you. Except he has to use a plane."

"Um, Artie?" Tweed raised an eyebrow. "You do realize that you're talking to a gargoyle, right?"

"What?" He blinked. "Oh! Huh. How 'bout that. I guess my supernatural translating powers are still in good working order! That Zahara-Safiya was a real peach!"

"Do I even want to know what he's talking about?" Feedback asked warily.

"Artie got himself cursed by an ancient Egyptian mummy princess named Zahara-Safiya a while back and she made him her minion translator." Cheryl shrugged. "So, in answer to your question, no. Probably not."

"That's what I thought," Feedback murmured.

"Okay, look," Pilot said. "This is serious. We're trapped in here. Now, I know C and T here are flying out of radar range. And *I* didn't say anything to anyone 'cause I didn't want them getting in heck. So, Karl ... did you tell *your* parents about coming out to this crazy contest in the middle of nowhere?"

"Heck, no." Feedback shook his head. "I mean, they probably wouldn't have cared, but I figured, why take the risk? I just snuck out of my room after dinner."

Pilot sighed deeply. "So ... *nobody* other than us knows we're here."

"*I* know," Artie said.

"Yeah," Tweed said, "but you're here."

"So?"

"Did *you* tell anyone else you were coming here?" Cheryl asked hopefully.

"Heck, yes I did!" Artie exclaimed, looking exceptionally proud of himself.

The twins exchanged a glance. Maybe they weren't doomed after all. Maybe someone would come looking for them ...

"Who exactly did you tell, Art-Bart?" Pilot asked.

"I told you!"

"And where am I?"

"Don't be dumb, Armbruster!" Artie snorted. "You're right here!"

"Yup. I am."

"And I ... oh." Artie's snort turned into something of a nervous coughing fit.

An uncomfortable silence descended as the lot of them looked back and forth at each other wondering just what the heck they were supposed to do now. Then Feedback's head snapped up and his expression brightened right up. For a second, the girls thought that maybe he'd thought of a way out of their predicament, but that wasn't it.

"*Super* cool!" he exclaimed, pointing to the pile of gear Tweed had emptied out of her knapsack to get to her Nerf bow. "What is *that*?"

Apparently, where the tech-prodigy babysitter was concerned, all heebie-jeebies and life-and-limb concerns were automatically put on hold in the face of unfamiliar technology. In this case, a Drive-In speaker.

Cheryl nudged Simon with the toe of her sneaker. "That's … kind of hard to explain," she said. "His name is Simon. He's—"

"He's awesome!" Feedback enthused, crossing the room with a bounce in his step to get a closer look. "This metal housing is totally retro tech! It's got, like, a steampunk vibe!"

"Help!" Simon exclaimed as Feedback picked him up and started to turn him over and over, juggling him from hand to hand and examining him with a critical eye. "Unhand me! I'm prone to motion sickness!"

"That's hilarious!" Feedback held the speaker up to his eye and peered through the grate, trying to see inside. "You hid a wireless receiver in it? Is it digital?" He spun the speaker around again and squinted at the wire opening.

"How rude!" Simon squawked.

Artie snorted with laughter.

"Radical!" Feedback's grin widened and he flipped the speaker over to peer at its backside. "Who's operating the transmitter?"

"Uh, *Simon* is," Cheryl said and plucked the speaker from Feedback's clever fingers before the disembodied spirit of the deceased mystic began to make spectral barfing noises. "He's kind of … transmitting from the beyond, I guess."

"Beyond … huh?" Feedback's cheery grin faltered. "You mean it's not digital?"

"Definitely not," Tweed said.

She and Cheryl exchanged glances. *Should we?* they wondered.

The last thing they wanted to do was spill the beans about Simon Omar. But it was starting to look like they didn't have much choice. And, after all, they were already hip-deep into sharing a paranormal experience with the other sitter, anyway. The gargoyle prowling the perimeter of the haunted room was more than enough proof of that.

Also? Pilot was silently staring at them, waiting for an explanation.

"Told you," Cheryl muttered at him, recalling how he hadn't believed them earlier when they'd shown him the speaker back at C+T headquarters.

"When Cheryl says 'beyond,'" Tweed said, "she really *means* 'beyond.' Like, 'afterlife' kind of beyond."

"Oh, not again!" Pilot threw his hands in the air.

Feedback started to blink rapidly, as if his brain was frantically trying to process information input that simply did not compute. "Wait. Is this like the flying bat-cat thing?" He glanced warily at the gargoyle who sat scratching at one ragged ear with its sharp-taloned back foot.

"No, no, no," Tweed said with an air of authority on the subject. "Well, yes. Sort of. It's technical. I mean, the speaker is definitely possessed. But that's only because we opened up the trans-dimensional portal for the ancient Egyptian mummy princess we told you about to cross over into her afterlife. You see, the mystical shockwave seems to have activated the dormant spectrally enhanced personality of a kablooied mystical magician guy from the turn of the century named Simon Omar, whose spirit force was already trapped in a jewel on display in the curiosities tent at that carnival that rolled in and out of town last week. There's a fine distinction between *possession* and *haunting*. But it generally takes a supernatural connoisseur to distinguish between the two."

"Okaaaay ..." Feedback resumed edging toward the door. "I'ma gonna try and gedoutta here again ..."

"Good luck with that." Cheryl threw a jaunty wave in his direction. "I don't think any of us is going anywhere until the house decides it wants to let us."

Feedback stopped edging as he seemed to realize that the girls really *did* know what they were talking about, and that he was stuck in a situation that was weirder than anything he'd ever encountered. The only thing to do was not panic.

"Okay," he said, taking a deep, calming breath. "All right. One step at a time, right? Just like a video game. One level at a time. It's just a puzzle, right? If only we could figure out how to get out of this room ... then together maybe we could work to figure out the lock on the front door," he said. "There's a keyhole but I couldn't find a key. I worked at it for almost ten minutes with my handy-dandy battery-powered pocket screwdriver but I couldn't get that big bronze doorknob to budge—"

"Doorknob!" Simon piped up suddenly, startling them all and making Cheryl fumble and almost drop him. "Right! I *knew* there was something I was forgetting!"

"What's that?" Tweed asked.

"So, you know this house is haunted, right?" Simon asked smugly, as if he hadn't been paying attention to a thing they'd said and just assumed they didn't know that at all.

"Well, duh." Cheryl rolled an eye at the speaker. "That *was* kind of the conclusion we came to, yeah."

"Oh." He sounded a bit deflated, like they'd beat him to the punchline of a joke he was telling.

"Okay, okay," Cheryl relented. "I'll bite. What do you know about this house and the specifics of the spookificationing thereof, Speakie?"

"Well, it's not so much about the *house*. It's more about the *doorknob* of the house, really." Simon's voice brightened up considerably. "You know. Seeing as how it was part of Dudley's World-O-Wonders curiosities exhibit and all."

"*What?*" Cheryl's expression darkened at the mere mention of that charlatan Colonel Dudley and his travelling sham-show. She opened her mouth to express her opinion in impolite terms but Tweed silenced her with a raised hand.

"Go on," she encouraged the speaker.

"Right," Simon Omar continued. "Well. The thing's been sitting in a glass case right next to my turban jewel for years!"

"The Spirit Stone of Simon Omar?" Tweed raised an eyebrow. "You're kidding."

"I'm not!" Simon protested. "That big old bronze knob was found in the ruins of a manor house in Yorkshire, England, that once belonged to some rich old nutcase."

"Ruins?" Tweed asked.

"Yup," the speaker said. "Much like yours truly, that house blew itself to smithereens!"

"What happened?" Feedback asked.

"Couldn't say," Simon said with a vocal shrug. "I only caught bits and pieces of the story by way of carnival-attendee chatter."

Cheryl blinked at the speaker for a minute, and then tossed it over to Tweed and shrugged out of her knapsack again. "Hang on …"

She dug around in the front pocket and emerged with the handful of typewritten index cards that the twins had collected from the place where the curiosities exhibit tent had stood in the field after the World-O-Wonders carnival had bugged out of town. Tweed briefed Feedback on the carnival leftovers the girls had collected while Cheryl shuffled through the cards until she found the one she was looking for.

"Eureka!" she exclaimed and held it aloft triumphantly. When Feedback and Tweed and Artie and Pilot crowded around to see, she held the card out so they could read the faded words. "Check it out, guys!"

"Hey!" Simon's muffled protest sounded from the crook of Tweed's elbow. "I can't see!"

Tweed rolled her eyes and shifted the speaker, holding it up so that the glare from the Spirit Stone illuminated the card.

HECKLESTONE MANOR DOORKNOB
The only remaining artifact from a stately Victorian manor house, once owned by wealthy eccentric scientist and dabbler in the OCCULT, Sir Hector Hecklestone. Rumours abounded that Hecklestone was cursed by his arcane experiments with ECTOPLASM, having lost his wife to a freak lightning strike and, some years later, all three of his children when the manor house inexplicably exploded when Sir Hector was abroad!!
THE TERROR! THE HORROR! THE TRAGEDY!

"Right!" the departed mystic said. "That's it. I remember now. Dudley would yammer on and on to carnival-goers about how the antiques dealer he bought the knob from had sworn he could hear the thing whispering and giggling dementedly in the middle of the night."

"Boy, there sure was an awful lot of exploding going on back in your day," Artie said.

"Well, that kind of thing sometimes happens when mystical convergences go sideways," Simon said. "Occupational hazard. With Hecklestone, it was all about the ectoplasm."

"Ecto-what-now?" Artie raised an eyebrow at him.

"Ectoplasm. Residue from the astral plane."

Cheryl and Tweed nodded in sage understanding.

"Hecklestone was convinced it was an untapped renewable energy resource," Simon said. "Kind of like ... crude oil with a spectral kick."

"Wow." Feedback shook his head. "The Victorians were really kind of weird." He glanced at the speaker. "Er. No offence, Mr. Omar."

"None taken," Simon said graciously. "Totally agree. Most of us were absolute nutters! You see, back in the day, folks didn't really distinguish between magic and science the same way you lot seem to now," he explained. "I mean, Thomas Edison, that great scientific inventor, called himself the Wizard of Menlo Park and was forever yammering on about inventing a spirit phone to talk to the dead! He could have just come to one of my shows!"

"I read somewhere that people thought that inventor dude Nikola Tesla was either some kind of a sorcerer or was using technology from aliens," Feedback said with a disbelieving snort. "I mean, seriously. UFOs?"

Cheryl and Tweed exchanged a glance, but under the circumstances, they thought that correcting Feedback's misconceptions about the subject of extraterrestrials would probably just overload the poor kid's brain circuits. So they kept quiet and listened as Simon continued.

"Oh, no," said the mystic speaker. "Tesla was just really good at math. But like I said, it was hard to tell the difference."

"You coulda told us this Heckle-stuff earlier, y'know." Cheryl glowered at the speaker. "Like before we actually set foot inside this house."

"I tried to tell you!" Simon protested. "You stuffed me in a bag."

"Yeah? That was ages ago. You could have piped up since then."

"I told you, I forgot." His voice turned sulky. "I forget a lot of things. And speaking of ages, I've been dead for several of them and *you're* criticizing my faulty memory? Very sensitive."

"All right, all right. Don't pout!" Cheryl sighed. "We're here now. We just have to figure out how to get *not* here. So … first things first. Can somebody please tell me—what the heck is a doorknob from a 'sploded house in England doing attached to the door of a house in Wiggins Cross?"

Tweed put a finger in the air, silencing her cousin again, while she knit her forehead in a fierce frown beneath her dark bangs. Cheryl recognized the signs: Tweed was having a brainwave. But she held her tongue.

"Okaaaay," Tweed mused. "Let's think about this. On the one hand, we have the jewel from a turban, containing the actual trapped spirit of a magician who dabbled in the occult—"

"I was hardly a dabbler!"

"Shh!" Cheryl put a hand over the speaker's grille.

"— and who is able now to manifest after the Egyptian portal explosion shot out a wave of arcane energy ..." Tweed continued, ignoring the mystic's protest. "What if, on the *other* hand, we now have a doorknob that was also *actually* likewise inhabited by the spirits of the departed—in this case, the Hecklestone kids, victims of the aforementioned explodination. What if that same Egyptian mystical energy wave activated them the same way? Simon can talk now because the speaker allows him to. What if there was, say, an old house already sitting on this chunk of land when the portal blew? What if the Dudley doorknob landed on it, embedding itself in the same way Simon Omar's Spirit Stone fused with our Drive-In speaker?"

"And the paranormal energy that was released from the doorknob rebuilt the house in the image of its former self!" Feedback exclaimed, following the logic of Tweed's theory.

"And provided an environment in which to contain its former occupants ..." Tweed nodded and glanced around the room, half-expecting to see the three Hecklestone kids listening in on the conversation. But if they were, she couldn't tell. "If the emanations were strong enough, they might very well have altered the surrounding plot of land. And more! Do *you* ever remember an Eerie Lane in Wiggins before now, Feedback?"

"Nope. I even tried to dial it up on my phone's GPS, but all I got was random pixels." He snorted in derision. "I had to look at an old-fashioned paper map to get here—and it was so faded I almost missed finding this place. Now I wish I had."

"Gah!" Cheryl shuddered, thinking about the weird and wacky assortment of objects that she and her cousin were unintentionally responsible for scattering around the town. "Those carnival Duds shot all over Wiggins," she said. "Do you mean to tell me that every single piece of dusty junk in that tent is now gonna come to life and mess with the town? We're gonna have to clear our schedule!"

Tweed frowned. "You could be right, partner. Hopefully it's not as bad as all that," she said. "I mean, as much of a scammer as Dudley was, most of that stuff was probably nothing more than dime-store trash. He probably just got lucky with a few authentic curiosities, and I don't think he realized that some of the exhibits in his collection *really were* the real thing. Not beyond the mummy princess, anyway. As it is, I'm pretty sure it's safe to say that Bob Ruth's softball isn't going to conjure up an army of ghostly baseball players or anything ..."

"I hope not!" Artie said. "I took that thing home— it's sitting on my nightstand—and I'd have a real tough time explaining *that* to my mom ..."

"Hey," Tweed said with a grin, "at least your tail and scales disappeared."

"Please." Artie ran a hand through his slicked-back hair and adjusted his glasses. "I *rocked* that croc."

Feedback had been silent for a few moments, just staring back and forth between the girls. Now he backed off a step, shaking his head. "Whoa," he said. "I'd heard you guys had radically unconventional sitter techniques. Now I'm just thinking you're radically unconventional about *everything*. Also? Kinda freaking me out."

"Don't worry about it." Cheryl flipped her pigtails back. "We train for situations like this."

"Train how?"

"Well ..." Tweed attempted to frame an explanation in a way that Feedback would understand. "You're always playing those zombie-smasher games, right?"

"Right," Feedback said warily.

"Well, if a real zombie apocalypse happened, you'd most likely have an advantage over regular, non-gamey people, right?"

"I guess ..."

"Well, it's kind of like that with us. We know monsters because we watch monster movies."

"They're like training videos with popcorn!" Cheryl grinned.

"Oh, man ... I could *totally* go for popcorn right now!" Feedback lamented.

Wordlessly, Tweed fished a chocolate-chip granola bar out of her knapsack and handed it over to Feedback, who seemed to have come to the Hecklestone Great Sitter Challenge expecting to raid the fridge in epic sitter style.

"Thanks!" he said, and unwrapped the bar, devouring it in only a few bites. "You know, it might sound kinda selfish, but I'm glad you guys are all trapped in here, too. I mean, I'd hate to be in here all by myself."

"I wonder if Cindy and Hazel are saying that very same thing right now," Tweed mused, wondering that the rival duo had yet to really put in an appearance.

Cheryl slapped the index card against her palm, lost in thought. "So ..." she said. "Ectoplasm, huh?"

"Yessiree," Simon said.

"Which is ... *what* again, exactly?" Pilot asked.

"Hard to describe," Simon said. "It's sort of a weird sticky residue they used to find at seances or in haunted houses. Evidence of the spirit realm left behind from close encounters with the astral plane."

"You know," Cheryl said, "ghost goop."

"Spectral slime," Tweed elaborated.

Artie grimaced. "Yuck."

"Like ... uh ... *that* stuff?" Feedback pointed to the corner of the room, where a creeping grey film of gelatinous goop was starting to drip menacingly from the ceiling.

10 THE LEAGUE OF AWESOME

"**P**lease tell me this is just one of the sitter challenges," Feedback said, backing away, wide-eyed, from the creeping ooze. "This place really isn't haunted. And that's not ecto-goop. It's just … Jell-O, right? Harmless, right?"

"Eeww …" Cheryl shuddered as a thick glop of ectoplasm hit the black-and-white carpet with a noise like a giant slug belching. The carpet began to sizzle and tendrils of vaporous smoke began to rise like fog. The stench was overwhelming—like rotten eggs and burnt rubber. "Challenging, yes," she said. "Harmless … I wouldn't go that far."

"We've gotta get outta here!" Tweed exclaimed.

"Look!" Artie pointed at the bookshelves behind them, which had been empty only moments earlier, but were now filled floor to ceiling with heavy, leather-bound books, bronze ornaments and scientific oddments. Where the little round table had been bare before except for a cloth covering it, there now sat a large, gleaming crystal ball on an elaborately decorative brass base.

"Holy moly," Cheryl said, pointing to the glassy globe. "The old Heckster must have held a whole buncha seances in here. This room is probably crawling with spectral whammitude ..."

"How are we going to get out of here?" Artie asked nervously.

"We'll have to work as a team!" Pilot said.

"I can't do that!" Feedback yelped. He'd gone very pale and was starting to shift nervously from foot to foot. "I'm a loner! I hate multi-player games!"

Cheryl and Tweed exchanged a glance with Pilot. They were going to have to figure out a way to keep Feedback from a complete meltdown.

"I got it! Grab our gear and follow my lead, guys ..." Cheryl whispered. Then she turned to Feedback and said, "D'you like superheroes, Feedback?"

"Of course I do," he said, almost climbing one of the suddenly stocked bookshelves in his anxiousness. "What self-respecting nerd doesn't like superheroes?"

"Well ... Batman's kind of a loner," Cheryl said, "and so's Superman, but they still get together with the Justice League sometimes, right?"

"I'm not a superhero."

"Not yet."

As the dripping ooze crept ever closer, Cheryl and Tweed explained the concept of ACTION!! to Feedback. Cheryl figured if they could take Feedback's mind off the realities of their present predicament, then maybe they could all work together to *solve* their present predicament.

"You got it?" Artie asked when the brief briefing wrapped up. He'd been a participant—willing and unwilling—in the twins' bouts of ACTION!! for years and knew the drill. So did Pilot.

"I think so ..." Feedback swallowed nervously.

"All right then." Cheryl nodded decisively. "Cameras rolling ... aaaaand ..."

"… *ACTION!!*"

EXT. THE ORBITING HEADQUARTERS OF THE LEAGUE OF AWESOME. Start of a classic "SUPERHERO TEAM ROLL-CALL SEQUENCE."

MUSIC BEGINS A SLOW BUILD. CAMERA CLOSE-UP on a HAND CLENCHING A MONKEY WRENCH FADING INTO VIEW (SFX: SPARKLY ATOM-TRANSPORTER EFFECT), ONE FINGER BEARS THE LoA INSIGNIA RING. AN IMPRESSIVE VOICE-OVER (I.V.O) VOICE IS HEARD.

> I.V.O.
> (impressively)
> Once a mild-mannered airplane
> mechanic by day …

CLOSE-UP shot as HANDSOME YOUNG MECHANIC turns to CAMERA and offers a grin, wink and thumbs-up …

> I.V.O.
> A freak lightning storm and a tank
> of experimental high-test jet fuel
> combined to create … *FLYBOY*!! He
> soars through the skies zapping evil
> with his Supersonic Monkey Wrench!

LIGHTNING FLASHES, revealing FLYBOY! In awesome winged costume and mask, brandishing a GLOWING WRENCH.

> FLYBOY
> (in "catch-phrase" voice)
> Fly the friendly skies!!

ATOM-TRANSPORTER SPARKLE is activated
again ... revealing a hand, holding a
SMARTPHONE with a screen showing detailed
techno-schematics, wearing the LoA insignia
ring.

> I.V.O.
> (impressively)
> Super-genius, tech-startup multi-
> gajillionaire by day ...

CLOSE-UP shot of HIP, FUNKY YOUNG DIGITAL
ENTREPRENEUR, thumbs a-blur, tapping away on
the screen of his device. He makes a FIST,
presses his LoA RING to the screen, and GREEN
ENERGY CRACKLES UP HIS ARM! ...

> I.V.O.
> He dedicated his life, super-genius-
> brain and gajillions of dollars to
> goodness, fair play and evil-bashing.
> He is *LITHIUM!* Battery-powered pro-
> TECH-tor of the people!

DIGI-ARMOUR encases his lanky frame, FLESH
AND TECH BLENDING TOGETHER INTO ONE AWESOME
CYBERNETIC SUPER-DUDE.

CAMERA CUTS TO CLOSE-UP of his glowy-eyed
helmet, which almost seems to wink.

> LITHIUM
> (in "catch-phrase" voice)
> Level ... *UP!!*

ATOM-TRANSPORTER SPARKLE is activated again ... revealing the girlish, freckled knuckles of a hand, clenched in a fist, wearing the LoA insignia ring.

> I.V.O.
> (impressively)
> Dynamic, spitfire tomboy to her friends, no one knows the monstrous secret that lurks beneath her freckled skin ...

CLOSE-UP shot of PRETTY, PERKY, FRECKLED YOUNG LASS, TEETH BARED IN A SCARY GRIMACE.

> I.V.O.
> A million-dollar movie stunt gone wrong, an unmarked toxic waste dump and a hopelessly lost transport truck fully loaded with illegal fireworks combined to create ... *THE TOXIC REVENGER!!*

> TOXIC REVENGER
> (in "catch-phrase" GROWL)
> KA-BLAAAAMO!!

ATOM-TRANSPORTER SPARKLE is activated yet
again ... revealing a pale hand with a black
lacquered manicure, fingers splayed, wearing
the LoA insignia ring.

                    I.V.O.
          •
                 (impressively)
          Adventurous expert in the occult,
          on a journey to investigate an
          archaeological find in a spider cave
          deep in the Amazon jungle --

                 OFF-CAMERA VOICE
                 (interrupting)
          I don't like where this is going --

                    I.V.O.
                 (more impressively)
          This shy young lass was bitten by a
          highly venomous, conveniently mutated
          super-spider --

                 OFF-CAMERA VOICE
                 (interrupting)
          Seriously?? I'm not --

                    I.V.O.
              (even more impressively)
          Only to become TARANTU-LASS!!

                 TARANTU-LASS
             (glowering at TOXIC REVENGER)
          A spider? We need to talk.

                 TOXIC REVENGER
              (giving a brutish thumbs-up)
          RAAAGGHRR!!

ATOM-TRANSPORTER SPARKLE is activated yet one
last time ... revealing a white-gloved hand
beneath a crisp cuff, embellished with an
elegantly stylish cufflink. The LoA insignia
ring is visible on one gloved finger as
another gloved hand tugs the cuff straight
beneath a stylish jacket sleeve.

                    I.V.O.
                (impressively)
        Suave, mysterious, impeccably dressed
        and a hit with the ladies in all
        the best nightclubs, he is Mister
        Mysterioso, Master of Shadows!

CLOSE-UP SHOT of a debonair face, half-
shrouded in shadows and wearing a black mask
over his eyes. He WINKS at the camera.

                    I.V.O.
        With his winged-minion companion at
        his side, Mister Mysterioso commands
        the Power of the Night!

                MISTER MYSTERIOSO
        (in super-suave "catch-phrase" voice)
        Say good night, evildoers. It's past
        your bedti -- GLAACK!!

CLOSE-UP SLO-MO SHOT OF MISTER MYSTERIOSO
GETTING UNEXPECTEDLY SMACKED RIGHT IN THE
KISSER BY A BIG OL' LEATHER-BOUND BOOK!!

            TARANTU-LASS AND TOXIC REVENGER
        Cut! CUT!! Cut! CUT!!

"CUT!! ..."

"Artie!" Tweed yelped at the sight of him flat on his back, with his glasses knocked off and his nose buried—literally!—in a book.

"Shrimpcake!" Cheryl exclaimed. "Are you okay?!"

"Who did that?" came the pained, muffled reply. "Also ...? Ow."

"Hey!" Feedback exclaimed as the corner of an encyclopedia volume grazed his shoulder. Another one narrowly missed his head.

The French doors slammed shut and books flew through the air, banging against them with loud heavy thuds that didn't break the thick glass, but left behind splotches of ectoplasmic glop dripping down the panes. A heavy brass kaleidoscope launched itself off its oak stand and nearly took Cheryl's eye out! She shoved Simon back in the pack for safety and dropped to crouch on all fours.

"And Hecklestone thought he could control this stuff?!" she exclaimed, covering her head. Books and paperweights and decorative knick-knacks continued to zip perilously through the air, smashing into walls and windows in explosions of sticky ecto-glorp. "Sure! What could *possibly* go wrong?"

"Whoa!" Pilot exclaimed as a copy of *Olsen's Standard Book of British Birds* ricocheted off the fireplace mantel, exploding in a cloud of flapping pages. "A little light reading, guys?"

Ramshackle looped and dove above Artie's head, batting away a flurry of flying tomes as Artie scrambled to find his glasses and staggered to his feet. The gargoyle's off-kilter manoeuvres actually seemed to help him avoid getting pummelled by the literature, and he was hissing angrily and meow-barking at the projectile-launching bookcases.

"We've *seriously* got to get out of here!" Tweed exclaimed, crab-crawling her way across the floor toward her cousin. "Before a rogue dictionary pulverizes one of us into alphabet soup!"

"Or we're smothered in ecto-goop!" Cheryl agreed.

"The door's still locked!" Feedback shouted as he kicked at it. "Jammed tight! What do we do?"

Cheryl and Tweed exchanged a glance. It seemed as if the ghost house had pretty specific ideas as to which way they should go. There was, after all, only *one* way out of that room that wasn't a door or a window or a locked-from-the-other-side secret staircase.

"An old stage magician's trick it is, then," Tweed said grimly.

"We don't know what's down there!" Cheryl protested.

"No. But we know what's up here."

The sounds of ectoplasm SPLAT-SIZZLE were almost louder now than the sounds of book and knick-knack impacts. Options were limited.

"All right, all right," Cheryl muttered nervously. "Here's hoping for laundry chute over tiger pit ..."

"Here's hoping!" Tweed agreed fervently. When

Cheryl hesitated, Tweed gripped her by the shoulder. "We can do this, partner. Just think of it as another challenge! After all, you're the Toxic Revenger, right? And I'm … I'm …"

Cheryl blinked at her, waiting.

"I'm Tarantu-lass!" Tweed said, finally.

Cheryl grinned fiercely. "You are?"

"I am!" Tweed said decisively. "And we're founding members of the League of Awesome!"

That was all it took. That moment of decisiveness. The girls exchanged the C+T Secret Signal (patent pending) and Cheryl spun around to see the boys on the other side of the room in various poses of crouch/ huddle/flying-book-avoidance.

"Right! Okay, League!" Cheryl called. "Hit the dirt! Stay low! Don't stop! And follow us!"

Crawling on her elbows, Cheryl slithered across the floor like a snake in a shooting gallery. When she got to the square in the carpet that marked the trap door, she shifted all her weight forward and heard a surprised yelp from Feedback as she tumbled forward and vanished.

Tweed followed close behind. As the twins disappeared headfirst into darkness, they heard the boys dropping to the floor and scurrying in their wake.

"If this was a video game," Feedback lamented, "I'd be online looking for cheat codes right now! This is craaaaaaaazy ………"

11 THE MAGNIFICENT ~~TWO~~ ~~THREE~~ ~~FIVE~~ SEVEN

One by one, Cheryl, Tweed, Pilot, Artie and Feedback fell headfirst through the trap door, down a steeply angled narrow passage and out into a gloomy, cavernous room in a rain of books and knick-knacks. One by one, they tumbled out onto a bare stone floor. Groaning and rubbing at a variety of bruised knees and elbows, the quintet slowly got to their feet and looked around.

As Feedback stood, the last of the books that had accompanied them on their mad dash down the chute dropped on his head, sending up a little cloud of dust. Feedback sneezed loud enough to rattle the small, barred windows set high up in the walls. They were, quite obviously, in the basement of the house. Feedback sneezed again.

"A-zoom-tight!" Artie said.

"I think you mean *gesundheit*, Art-Bart," Pilot said, straightening his hat.

"I'm not up on my Greek." Artie waved the matter away, and turned to examine the opening they'd all just tumbled through. Which was, of course, now closed. "Guess we'd better start looking for another way out again. Again."

Artie bent down and picked up a book. It looked to be the one that had initially bashed him in the beak and he glared at it reproachfully. But, realizing that it was hefty enough to use as a bashing implement in case of another spectral attack, he tucked it under his arm. Then he turned and started knocking on walls and pipes and squinting at cracks in the plaster with one eye squeezed shut.

"Hey, guys?" Feedback stopped Cheryl and Tweed for a moment. "Uh ... thanks."

"For what?" Tweed asked.

"For letting me in on that ACTION!! game thing. That was cool."

"No problem," Cheryl said. "We find it kinda helps get you motivated in situations like that one."

"Yeah. Yeah, it did. Like ... playing a video game, only for real." He grinned, looking a little more at ease. "And I've never had my own alter-ego and catch-phrase!"

They spread out, tentatively exploring the shadow-shrouded space. Truthfully, it did sort of look a bit like a laundry room, only without anything that even remotely resembled a modern washer/dryer set. A wide wooden doorway covered with a curtain was set into one wall. Cheryl pushed the curtain aside and then jumped back, in case something leaped out at them.

The curtain just swayed ominously in a non-existent breeze. But at least that was all that happened, for the time being. The twins stepped over the threshold into the other room, Feedback following close behind. He didn't really seem to want to let the twins out of his sight. The room beyond was dimly lit by the flickering purple glow of a half-dozen or so clear glass globes filled with fiery, dancing filaments of energy that looked like lightning captured in a ball. They were scattered around the place, on stands or on the long tables that took up most of the space and held a vast jumbled assortment of wacky-looking, mad-scientist-y, laboratory equipment.

"Coooool!" Feedback said, trotting over to the nearest light-ball, all thoughts of immediate peril once again driven from his techno-head at the prospect of examining some funky gadgetry. "These things are plasma globes! I tried to order one off the internet but my folks said it was a waste of my babysitter money."

He touched a fingertip to the curved surface of the glass globe, and the glowing filaments inside all gathered into one tendril and followed his fingertip around like an eager puppy. "You know you can power a fluorescent light tube just by touching it to the surface of one of these things?"

Cheryl and Tweed nodded absently as Feedback chattered excitedly. They might not have known the proper names or real-world applications for the weird fixtures scattered about the room, but they *instantly* recognized them as B-movie standard-issue mad-scientist-lab accoutrements—including a machine bristling with a pair of antennae that crackled with threads of electricity zipping upward at regular intervals. To Cheryl it looked like something right out of the lab from the original black-and-white Frankenstein movie, and it was surrounded on all sides by coiled glass tubes and beakers and flasks filled with greenish, smoking liquids, bubbling atop the Bunsen burners that furnished the room. In one corner, a bulky shape stood shrouded by a ghostly looking dropsheet. When Cheryl peeked beneath a corner of the cloth, all she could make out were cogs and wheels and gears and machine-y bits all half-jumbled together, mid-assembly, into some kind of diabolical-looking device.

"Well. If it isn't the Wiggins Weirdos," sneered a voice in the darkness.

The twins spun around to see Cindy Tyson and Hazel Polizzi standing half-hidden by a rack of test tubes filled with various coloured liquids.

"What are you two doing here?" Cindy asked accusingly, flipping one of her blonde braids back over her shoulder. It seemed less sleekly coiffed than usual and was starting to frazzle a bit like frayed rope at the end.

"Cindy ..." Hazel rolled her dark-brown eyes and nudged her sitter partner sharply with an elbow, murmuring, "Put a cork in it, okay? Maybe they're here to help us. And frankly? We could use it."

"But—"

"Seriously. We were in this house for, like, less than ten minutes when we fell down a trap door and couldn't get out."

"Oh. And they can?"

"Maybe." Cheryl shrugged.

"Right." Cindy's lip curled in a sneer. "*You* obviously fell for the trap door trap, too."

"Not exactly," Tweed said. "We knew it was there. We just used it as a door. Not a trap."

"I don't believe that for a second," Cindy muttered.

"It's true," Feedback said, stepping forward. "And they saved my butt in the process."

"Hey, Karl," Hazel said, attempting to muster up an appropriate level of adversarial-ness. "Never really expected to see you hanging out with the loony two. Couldn't handle the Great Sitter Challenge on your own?"

"Hey, Hazel," he said back, "I never really expected to either. But I think I picked a pretty good team to be on. *They* were smart enough to bring granola bars, at least."

Hazel's lips pressed into a thin smile and she stepped to one side gesturing to a substantial pile of crimped, brightly coloured paper cupcake wrappers, all empty, and several prettily decorated biscuit tins that contained nothing but crumbs and crumpled bits of waxed paper.

Did *all* the other sitters in town head to their gigs on empty, growling stomachs with the prospect of epic kitchen raids in mind? the twins wondered.

"Sitter challenge number one," Hazel said. "Locate and acquire provisions. Accomplished in style."

"I guess that was before you fell through the trap door, huh?" Tweed asked dryly. "Which number's that one again?"

Cindy opened her mouth and looked like she was about to snark a comeback, but just then, Artie and Pilot walked through the door. "Who is *that*?" she whispered to Hazel, giving her a sharp elbow nudge.

"That's Yeager Armbruster," Hazel said, raising an eyebrow. "You know him."

"Not him!" Cindy's eyes were wide and glittering in the flickering light. "The handsome one in the snappy threads."

Cheryl blinked at her, having heard the exchange. "You ... you're *kidding*, right?"

Artie obviously had heard, too. "Good eeEEee-ven-ing, ladies," he drawled. "The name's Bartleby. Arthur Bartleby."

It was as if he couldn't decide if he was playing the part of wickedly charming Transylvanian royalty or James

Bond. But he tucked the leather-bound book suavely under his arm and sauntered forward to lean indolently anyway.

"I don't believe we've met." Cindy took a step forward, extending a hand and actually batting her eyelashes.

"Oh, of *course* you have!" Tweed huffed in exasperation. "It's Artie Bartleby from Bartleby's Gas & Gulp! Everyone in Wiggins knows him."

Cindy did a double take. "Artie ..."

Artie shot Tweed a glare and laughed offhandedly, with a casual wave in the twins' direction. "Arthur, please," he corrected. "It's been ages, my dear. How have you been?"

Cindy blushed and blinked in confusion while the twins rolled their eyes and Pilot and Feedback exchanged shrugs.

"Hey," Feedback said after a moment. "Now that we're all here, we should work together to find a way out, don't you all think?"

Cindy tore her gaze away from Artie. "Oh, no!" she exclaimed. "We don't need *their* help. No way!"

"I dunno, Cindy." Hazel shifted uncomfortably. "We might not like it, but they might actually be better at this kind of stuff than we are."

"Not better," Cheryl said, making an honest effort to sound like she really meant it. "We, uh ... we just have different methods, is all."

Tweed nodded only a little reluctantly and attempted

an encouraging smile that was just a little bit of a pained grimace. "That's right," she said. "It doesn't mean we can't work together—"

"Yes it does!" Cindy protested hotly. "This is *supposed* to be a challenge. We're *supposed* to be in competition!"

"Says who, Cindy?" Hazel sighed wearily. "Some guy we haven't even met? Who's locked us in this weirdo house? I mean, what's the deal with this Hecklestone dude anyway? How do we even know that there *is* a Hecklestone dude?"

"Oh, there's definitely a Hecklestone dude," Feedback said. "At least, there was. He died a long time ago."

"And so, what?" Cindy snorted and crossed her arms over her chest. "You're going to tell us that he's haunting this place?"

"No." Tweed shrugged. "Something is, but we don't think it's him. We think maybe—"

Suddenly, a whisper of eerie sounds shivered through the air, interrupting Tweed's explanation. "*Naugh*-ty, *naugh*-ty ..." the voices, high and piping, said in singsong tones. "Daddy won't be *hap*-py ... Not *a*-llowed down in the *lab*-ora-tory ..."

"Why do creepy ghost children always have English accents?" Cheryl asked.

"Same reason they always do that creepy nursery-rhyme-singsong thing," Tweed said. "Because it's creepy."

"It's a cliché," Pilot said uneasily.

"It's not a cliché, it's a time-honoured *trope*, Flyboy," Cheryl said, even as she crossed her arms and glared at the empty air.

Cindy and Hazel had shrunk back into the corner of the laboratory. "Uh ... who's doing that?"

"Your babysitting subjects," Pilot said dryly.

"What?" Hazel glared at him, wide-eyed. "No way. This was supposed to be a straight-up house-sitting gig. No brats. This place is supposed to be empty!"

"It is," he elaborated. "Except for the ghosts haunting it, that is."

"That's seriously not funny!" Cindy fumed. "It's just some stupid trick!"

"Yup. Played on us by the dearly departed Daphne, Edwina and Roderick," Tweed said. "Tragic, really, the old Hecklestone family curse ..."

"Curse?" Cindy swallowed nervously and glanced around.

"Curse, shmurse," Artie said, stepping forward and waving the matter away with the flick of one hand. "Stick with me, little lady. I know my way around curses."

"This from a guy who was once whammied into a lizard," Cheryl muttered.

Tweed snorted in grim amusement.

"Crocodile," Artie muttered back out of one side of his mouth while he attempted to retain his suave grin on the other side. "And *ix-nay* on the *ammy-whay*. No reason to alarm the other ladies, girls ..."

Cheryl rolled her eyes and Tweed murmured, "So *we're* girls now and *they're* ladies? Pff."

Artie ignored her and turned back to the rival sitters. "It's just a big old empty house. Nothing to worry about."

"Except the ghosts," Hazel muttered sarcastically, but she didn't quite sound convinced that her sarcasm was entirely warranted.

"I'm on your side, Cindy," Artie said.

"Really, Arthur?" Cindy gazed at him with doe eyes.

Cheryl made a gagging noise and Artie shot her a glare.

"Absolutely!" He launched into a leisurely stroll around the lab, plucking up random instruments as he went, and tossing them back onto the work tables in a show of casual nonchalance. "I don't think we have anything to worry about, my friends," he said airily. "Three sadly departed kids with goofy old names. *Roderick?* I wonder if they called him 'Rowdy Roddy'! And *Daphne?* I bet it was 'Hey, Daffy!' around the schoolyard for her."

Cheryl and Tweed exchanged a worried glance with Pilot. It somehow didn't seem like a good idea to taunt their haunting hosts, even if it was Artie's way of trying to put the others at ease.

"And how about that Edwina?" he continued. "Maybe she was 'Fast Eddie.' Or 'Eddie Munster.' Or maybe—OW!!"

The others turned to see Artie hopping on one foot and rubbing his shin.

"Stupid stool!" He glowered at the work stool he'd run into. "Where'd you come from?" Then he seemed to notice Cindy staring at him with a worried look on her face. "Heh. I mean … how clumsy of me …" Artie kicked the stool sharply with the toe of his shiny borrowed shoe, which had probably belonged to the goofily named Roderick at one time.

The stool screeched back across the floor and slammed into Artie's other shin.

"OW! Why you—" He brandished the book he was still carrying like a club. "Cut it out, you creepy little brats!"

The flickering lights in the plasma globes suddenly brightened and flared in time with Artie's angry exclamation. The faint outlines of three shadowy figures zipped across a bare wall at the far end of the room and the giggling continued, alternating between manic and mournful-sounding.

"Wait," Hazel said coldly. "I see what's going on here. Don't fall for Mr. Charm School, Cindy—he's nothing but a clever distraction."

"What?" Cindy frowned at Artie in uncertainty.

"And I know why Karl's with them. He's the AV Club president at school, isn't he? With access to all kinds of speakers and projectors and stuff like that? I bet they cheated. I bet they got here before we did and set all this up. I bet if you turned that stool over, there'd be fishing line attached to the legs."

Cheryl and Tweed noticed that she didn't exactly back up her assertions by doing that, but never mind. The rivals were on a roll.

"That's it! That's what this is all about, isn't it?" Cindy took up the anti-haunting rant, eyes narrowing as she turned a nova-watt glare on the twins. "This isn't funny! We're trying to win this contest fair and square and you two weirdos and your accomplices pull this kind of spooky stuff to try and get us off our game!"

"We don't have to try to get you off your game!" Cheryl glared back. "You've got nothing on us and you know it! The only thing *you* two are is *this* tall to ride this ride!" She thrust her hand out like the carnival ride sign the twins had stashed back home in the barn.

Cindy blinked at Cheryl in confusion, her lip curling. "What on earth is *that* supposed to mean, freak?"

Pilot glanced nervously around the room. "Ladies …"

Neither Cheryl nor Cindy had noticed that the liquids in some of the beakers had started to bubble at a fever pitch. Two of them had boiled over, spilling onto the counter and leaving oozing puddles of what looked like the same sort of ectoplasmic glorp the League of Awesome had encountered in the library. Equipment started to rattle and shimmy across the surfaces of the work tables and the flickering tendrils of luminescence in the plasma balls were dancing crazily in time with the girls' verbal volleys.

"It *means*," Cheryl said, "that the only reason you guys get more gigs than us is because you were lucky enough to be born a few months earlier! That's what!"

"Oh, really?" Cindy jammed her fists on her hips and thrust out her jaw. "Maybe it has something to do with the fact that you two are weirdos! Weirdos too weird even for the 'aliens' to take away, right, Hazel?"

Hazel winced.

Cheryl gasped.

"Cindy!" Artie's jaw dropped in astonishment.

"Take that back, Cindy Tyson," Pilot said, teeth clenched. "Or so help me …"

Feedback tried to diffuse the situation with a "Hey … guys? Can't we just—"

And Tweed—in what would normally be typically *Cheryl*-like fashion—suddenly launched herself across the lab with a growl, arms outstretched, hands grasping for Cindy Tyson's neck! Cindy screamed and would have ducked out of the way, except she didn't need to.

No one seemed to have noticed that, over the fever pitch of the babysitters' argument, the singsong ghost voices had gone from rhyming ditties and creepy laughter to gale-force howling. As Tweed lunged, a sudden spectral tornado spun in from the four corners of the room, wrapped tightly around the shrieking form of Cindy Tyson and yanked her from Tweed's reach. The wind whirled the hapless sitter across the length of the laboratory, rattling tubes and beakers in its wake, and flung Cindy like a rag doll into the waiting maw of one of the enormous steamer trunks, built to transport lab equipment, that stood open and empty in the corner of the lab. The riveted steel lid of the heavy-duty trunk slammed shut with a booming, doomy thud. Then the three latch-locks on the trunk sprang to life and clacked shut like teeth gnashing.

The entire room went suddenly still and pin-drop silent.

After a long moment, from the pocket of Cheryl's knapsack, Simon Omar made a sound like nervously clearing his throat. "Well," he said. "That's not very good ..."

12 LOCKED AND GOADED!

Hazel stared frozen in wide-eyed horror at the steamer trunk. They could hear the faint sounds of Cindy pounding on the inside of the lid. "Cindy!" Hazel shouted suddenly. "Cindy!! Get *out* here! Don't you leave me alone with these weirdos!!"

Tweed picked herself up off the floor, where she'd landed in her missed leap for Cindy. The surge of rage that swept through her at Cindy's taunting had washed completely away in the face of the ghostly twister, and all that was left was a worried shadow in her grey eyes.

The same worry was mirrored in Cheryl's blue ones.

"Sorry about that, everybody," Tweed said quietly, smoothing her dark hair.

"Yeah," Cheryl said, yanking her pigtails straight. "Sorry ..."

"I probably should have mentioned that ghostly manifestations feed on negative energy, right?" Simon the speaker murmured from the pocket of Cheryl's knapsack.

"Yeah," she murmured back. "Thanks."

Pilot's head of steam had evaporated, too, in the wake of the spectral gale. "Okay, guys," he said, motioning to the twins and Artie and Feedback. "Huddle up." They gathered around in a tight circle. "We're gonna have to figure something out before Hazel completely freaks or Cindy suffocates."

"Pilot's right," Cheryl said. "It's up to us!"

Tweed nodded seriously. "It's okay," she said. "We're trained to handle situations like this. We just have to pool our sitter fu."

"Right," Feedback said. "We're gonna have to work as a team!"

"And we're gonna have to look for a crowbar," Artie suggested.

"If only I had internet access, I could Google 'how to open a locked trunk' ..." Feedback checked his phone and shook his head in frustration. He swallowed nervously and looked like he might be having a bit of a tough time keeping it together. "Maybe we could try that ACTION!! thing again—"

"Crowbar!" Artie was clearly in smashing mode.

"Maybe we should just look for the darn key!" Cheryl exclaimed.

"C'mon!" Tweed urged. "Everybody spread out. Check the shelves, the tops of cupboards, drawers, everywhere. Nobody keeps a trunk like that lying around unless they have the key."

The twins and their friends scattered throughout the room, searching frantically for a key that would open the trunk and let Cindy out. Nemesis or not, a fellow Wigginsian sitter was in peril, and C+T and Co. couldn't stand idly by! It felt as though a clock was ticking loudly as they searched and rummaged and ransacked and—

KLICK-*CLACK!*

The sound of the heavy steamer-trunk lock springing open made them all freeze. Cheryl and Tweed and Artie and Pilot and Feedback all turned to see Hazel crouched beside the trunk. Beside her, a leather pouch lay on the floor with a dozen or so thin metal implements spread out neatly.

Hazel Polizzi owned a professional lock-pick kit.

And she'd just used it to spring Cindy from her trunk.

Cheryl and Tweed stood there, open-mouthed.

"What?" Hazel shrugged nonchalantly. "Tools of the trade."

The twins exchanged a glance. How come *they* didn't have lock picks?

"Binky Barker is one of my regular sitter gigs," Hazel continued airily. "There isn't a room, car, cupboard or suitcase that kid hasn't locked herself into at one time or another. I travel equipped."

"Nice work," Tweed said, wide-eyed.

"Really nice." Cheryl nodded in agreement, a bit stunned.

It seemed now as though the sitter challenge really might be a real thing. And their rival had just seriously one-upped them. It was an uncomfortable sensation for the girls. If there was one thing they'd always had absolute faith in—beyond the truths conveyed to them by their beloved movies—it was their sitter skills. Even when the rest of the town seemed to go for the flashy, the fashionable, the ever-so-teeny-bit-older-than-them, they'd known in their hearts that they were the superior choice. But now ... lock picks? *Real* ones? Cheryl might have pretended once, during an espionage-themed ACTION!! sequence, to use a pair of chopsticks to pick a lock, but ...

"I ordered it off the internet," Hazel said, rolling up the kit and stuffing it into a pocket in her purse.

Feedback nodded knowingly.

"The only reason I couldn't pick us out of this stupid basement is because I couldn't find the stupid door!" She sniffed.

Suddenly the girls felt terribly uncertain. And ... young. Maybe they weren't the town's best sitters. Maybe thirteen *was* the magic age. Tweed and Cheryl exchanged uneasy glances as Artie rushed forward to offer Cindy a hand. But she shrugged away from him and climbed unsteadily to her feet unassisted, the breath heaving in and out of her lungs. She threw her hair back over her shoulders and looked like she might launch into a serious tirade for a moment, but then there was another sudden sound that made them all jump.

Thumpthump … thumpthumpthump … thump.

The thumpthumpthumping seemed to be coming from inside the walls.

"Oh, man," Feedback muttered. "What *now*?"

Cheryl and Tweed shook themselves from their moment of doubt and stepped forward, hauling out putter and Nerf dart-gun respectively. Pilot slid his new monkey wrench out of his overalls loop. Artie hefted the heavy leather book that had so effectively knocked *him* for a loop. Together, they took up defensive stances, shoulder to shoulder.

The other three sitters readily let them—none of them really having much experience in hand-to-hand combat—and waited for the next episode of weirdness to unfold. A tense silence descended on the subterranean laboratory. And then the wall made a noise that sounded like "MMrggwrgl?"

Artie elbowed Pilot and the twins aside and trotted up to lean against one of the walls, his ear pressed to the panelling.

"Mrgwllr?" he gurgled back. "Shack, buddy? That you? I was wondering where you'd got to …"

"What is that little nutcase doing?" Hazel asked, clearly not having succumbed to the charms of Artie's wardrobe makeover in the same way that Cindy had.

"GRrrwlrgggm ...?" Artie murmured, ignoring her. "Is there a trip lever? A latch or a button or something?"

"Art-Bart?" Pilot asked. "What are you—"

"It's Ramshackle!" Artie explained. "He's in the wall. He's been part of this house since it was built—er, y'know, before it exploded—"

"Before it *what?*" Hazel asked, baffled.

"—and he probably knows every nook and cranny and super-secret passageway!"

"Of which there seem to be *way* too many, if you ask me!" Feedback exclaimed. "Seriously! Who builds a place like this? What's wrong with using the front hall stairs?!"

Artie gargled a few more questions in Gargoyle and turned back to the others. "I asked him to see if he can open the passage for us ..."

"Who's Ramshackle?" Hazel asked, suspicious.

"A friend," Cheryl said before anyone could blurt out the exact species of that "friend." She somehow didn't think Hazel and Cindy would buy *that* story. "He's going to help us."

"I told you—we don't need your help!" Cindy glared mutinously.

In that instant, a section of wall panelling slid aside, revealing another spiral staircase leading upward. Tweed turned to Cindy, who wore an expression of blank astonishment on her face.

"Okay, then," she said with a small, grimly satisfied smile. "I guess we'll just be shutting this here hidden passageway behind us when we go and you can find your own."

"No!" Hazel cried. "Wait!"

"C'mon!" Artie exclaimed, bounding up the stairs two at a time.

The others followed hastily in his wake, just in case the wall decided to slide shut again. The top of the hidden staircase exited out through the front of a big old grandfather clock. Artie pushed open the false face of the timepiece and stepped into the living room/study, whispering to Ramshackle to strike a pose on the ornate mantel of the fireplace—where a pale-flamed fire now burned—and not move.

Cindy and Hazel came out next, having pushed past Cheryl and Tweed on the narrow spiral stair in their rush to escape the lab. As Cindy passed the fireplace, she looked up to see the gargoyle, doing his best impression of his stony daylight persona. She pulled a sour face and muttered, "What a creepy statue!"

Pilot was the last one up. He immediately started checking all the windows in the room. The big oak door in the marble foyer beyond was doubtless still locked but maybe one of the study windows would be open. No such luck. They were all latched tight, painted shut, and utterly unbudgeable. The fire burning in the fireplace discouraged trying to shimmy up the chimney—especially when it flared dramatically, hissing and popping like a living thing as Pilot approached the hearth.

"You know," he said with a sigh, "as much as I hate to advocate the destruction of personal property, I say we're gonna have to try to break a wind—"

"That's it! Outta my way!!" Cheryl bellowed as she tore past him, brandishing the heavy iron poker from the fireplace high over her head. "I've had enough of this hokey-pokey!"

"Does she mean *hocus-pocus*?" Feedback asked.

"Let her go, pal," Artie said. "She's on a roll."

Cheryl brought the poker crashing down onto the window glass—only to have it bounce right off!

"That's quality Victorian manor house window glass there, missy," Simon whispered at her from his concealment. "They don't make 'em like that anymore."

It was true. The pane was so thick its surface was rippled and hard to see through. But she hadn't even cracked it!

"Plus it's probably reinforced with ectoplasmic residue," he continued. "This whole house was reconstituted from nothing but a doorknob, remember. There's some pretty hefty mystic might that went into creating this place, and those windows are no exception.

I mean, I'm sure it makes for lower heating bills come the winter and all but—"

"I don't care!" Cheryl howled in frustration. "I don't plan on still being here in the winter! I don't plan on still being here in the *morning*!"

She bashed at the window a dozen more times but it was no use. In the silence that followed, the fire crackled with a sound like grim chuckling.

"Hey …" Feedback said, looking around. "Where are the other sitters?"

Cheryl and Tweed looked around. "They didn't fall through another trap door, did they?" Cheryl asked, not particularly upset by the prospect.

"Cindy?" Artie called. "Hazel?"

Silence.

Followed by the sound of a key turning in a heavy lock.

It came from the foyer of the house.

Cheryl and Tweed exchanged a glance and then ran for the grand front foyer, the boys hot on their heels. They were just in time to see Hazel, a fistful of lock picks clutched tightly in one hand, throw her arms up in the air in triumph.

"Yes!" Cindy pushed her out of the way and heaved open the door.

Scrambling over top of each other in their haste, the pair lurched over the threshold and out onto the porch—just as the enormous bronze doorknob began to glow to angry life! Cindy and Hazel screamed in fright, and over their panicked cries, the others heard the ghostly wailing sounds of the Hecklestone Trio of Terror crying out. But then the roar of a gale-force wind blotted out the cacophony of voices as it came boiling down the chimney flue and burst out of the gaping maw of the living-room fireplace like an invisible freight train. It rushed past, almost bowling the bunch of them over, and slammed the front door shut again!

With Cindy Tyson and Hazel Polizzi on the outside.

The doorknob was pulsing with furious spectral energy in glow-stick hues of goblin green, and when the sound of the lock tumbling back into place boomed through the house, it blazed like a beacon and then went dark. The keyhole glared like the empty eye socket in a skull and the twins knew, even without trying it, that the door would be locked up tight as a bank vault again.

The girls ran to the window on one side of the big oak door and looked out. The boys ran to the other. Out on the porch, Cindy and Hazel stood gasping, wild-eyed and crazy-haired.

"Hey! You guys can't just leave us here!" Feedback shouted.

"Yes, we can!" Hazel said, her voice muffled by the thick Victorian ecto-windows. "I *quit* this stupid contest! You win, you buncha cheater weirdos! And you can tell

Old Man Hecklestone we've got better things to do than to house-sit his creepy old mansion, anyway."

"Wait!" Artie pressed his hands up against the window beside the front door. "Cindy! I thought we had the start of a beautiful friendship!"

In the darkness lit only by the glow of the flickering porch lamp, Cindy's expression wavered for a brief moment. Then she shook her head, and through the thick glass, they heard her say, "Sorry, handsome! I'm looking out for number one! We're getting out of here. Good luck finding the fridge!"

Then she grabbed Hazel by the arm and dragged her off the porch, and the two of them tore down the path like a pack of ghouls was nipping at their heels.

"Huh …" Artie turned away from the window after they disappeared and Pilot put a consoling hand on his shoulder. "Dames." Artie snorted. "Right, Armbruster?"

"Right, Art-Bart." Pilot sighed wearily and wandered over to sit on the bottom step of the staircase. "Can't live with 'em."

"That's it?" Cheryl blinked, stunned by the suddenness of their rivals' departure. "We won?"

Tweed stared out the window with a faraway gaze, watching as the running shapes of Cindy and Hazel grew small in the distance at the end of the front yard path. "I guess we did," she said wonderingly. "I mean … it doesn't *feel* like winning …"

"No," Feedback said. "It kinda really doesn't."

"Can you guys please just forget about that stupid contest for a minute?" Pilot huffed in frustration. "Even if it was a real thing and not just something to lure you all here—which, he*llo*, it clearly *was*—you're all taking this matter of 'professional sitter pride' just a little too far!"

"I never thought I'd say this," Cheryl said, "but, Pilot, you're right."

"You never thought you'd say I was right?" He raised an eyebrow.

"No. About us taking our sitter business too seriously." She sighed. "Clearly Cindy and Hazel *do* have skills. And so do you, Feedback. We're not the only game in town. We shouldn't be."

"I didn't quite mean it like that, Cher-bear," Pilot said, putting an arm around her shoulders. "Of course you should take your business seriously. You're good at it—*great* at it—and you should be proud. What I meant was I think we need fewer super-sitters and more monster-mashers just at the moment!"

"Speaking as one of the aforementioned super-sitters," Feedback said, raising his hand, "I'll second that motion!"

The tension eased for a moment as the twins shook themselves out of their brief slump. One thing was for sure: the absence of Cindy Tyson and Hazel

Polizzi sure made things a whole lot quieter around the house.

Until Simon suddenly piped up brightly, saying, "Well, I'd say that was rather a lucky stroke of luck, eh, wot?"

"What was?" Cheryl asked, digging him out of the pocket of her knapsack.

"Getting that front door open like that."

"No it wasn't! We're still stuck here."

"Oh, no," the speaker explained. "Not for you. I meant, that was rather a stroke of luck for those girls. I mean, *they* timed it just right."

"They did?"

"Sure!" he said. "You probably distracted the house with your window bashing just long enough for them to jimmy open that door and escape. Doubt they would have managed it otherwise."

"Wait." Tweed put up a hand. "You think the *house* has a ... a what? A personality? Awareness?"

"Is that even possible?" Pilot asked. "I mean, do you *really* think an inanimate object can have a personality?" The speaker seemed to glare at him until Pilot realized what he'd just said. "Oh. Uh, sorry. No offence ..."

"I'd say it's a definite possibility," Simon said after another moment of silent glaring and a haughty sniff. "There was probably an enormous amount of ectoplasm soaked up by this house back in the day, what with

Hecklestone's experiments and seances and whatnot. Now, in the wake of *your* Egyptian-princess rescue, the resulting mystical ka-boom not only gave the house the power to reconstruct itself, it's also allowed it to take on a spectral life of its own."

"A spectral life with a really bad temper," Artie muttered, tossing the book that had conked him on the noggin onto a stair and slumping down beside it. Ramshackle appeared from the study and wandered over to head-butt him on the knee. Artie gave him a skritch behind his horn stubs and the little monster began to purr.

"Honestly," Simon continued in a scolding tone, "didn't anyone ever tell you people that messing around with otherworldly portals should only be handled by experts?"

"Um … *you* were an expert there, too, weren't you, Speakie?" Cheryl pointed out.

The glare from the Spirit Stone narrowed. "Thanks for the reminder."

"D'you think Cindy and Hazel will send help?" Artie wondered.

"Ha. I doubt it," Feedback scoffed, an expression of disdain curling his lip. "I know how those two operate and I'd bet my Xbox that they probably hoodwinked their folks, too, so they could come here tonight. They won't tell anyone 'cause they don't want anyone to know they were here!"

Cheryl frowned. "But …"

"Feedback's right, pal," Tweed said. "We know how competitive Cindy and Hazel are. And we know what they think about us."

"We're not *weird*," Cheryl grumbled.

"Sure we are!" Tweed said brightly (well, as brightly as she ever actually said anything). "And we should be proud of that. We're not like everyone else. And we're not like Cindy Tyson and Hazel Polizzi. We'd help them. I mean, we'd at least think about it."

Pilot shrugged. "I dunno. I'm inclined to cut 'em some slack on not sending help, *only* because I don't even think they think we're in really real trouble. You heard them. They think you two were behind all those spooky shenanigans just so you guys could win the sitter contest!"

"Arggh!" Cheryl screwed up her face and thrust Simon the speaker at Tweed. Her frustration at their entrapment boiling over again, she turned to pound on the door with both fists. Then with the fireplace poker. "Let us out, you haunted Heck House! Let! Us! OUT!!" The heavy oak planking shuddered beneath the blows and the doorknob began to glow angrily again. "LET US GO!!" she shouted as she continued her assault.

The others watched, astonished, until Ramshackle suddenly let out a loud "MrrORWrr!" and Cheryl froze, poker held high.

"What was that?" she asked, gasping for breath.

"He said, 'That's just what *they* keep saying,'" Artie said.

She turned and shot Artie a questioning look. He shrugged and bent an ear toward the little gargoyle and listened while the thing growled and grumbled. After a few moments, he turned back to the twins. "The kids—whatstheirnames—Ramshackle said that's what *they* keep saying."

"Let them out from where?" Tweed asked. "Seems to me they've been roaming free all over this old house!"

Ramshackle shook his head at the word *free*.

"Well ..." Tweed frowned. "If that's *not* the case, where are they now?"

The gargoyle turned to glare pointedly up the stairs as the angry green glow from the doorknob faded back to almost nothing. Cheryl gazed up the stairs and she remembered the dressing room—and the things she'd thought she'd seen, moving behind the mirror glass ...

"I think I know," she said. "C'mon, guys. We're gonna get to the bottom of this once and for all. Tweed? Follow me. Bring Speaker Boy."

"What are we going to do?" Tweed asked as she ran up the stairs beside her cousin.

"We're gonna take a page from Freddy and Marlene's movie script," Cheryl said.

"You mean *Ding Dong, You're Dead* Freddy and Marlene?" Tweed thought back to the hapless haunted couple in the movie they'd watched only the night before.

It seemed like ages ago. "You mean … we're going to scream and flail and generally run around like idiots?"

"Yup," Cheryl said, reaching the landing and turning left. The door to the library they'd been locked inside once again stood wide open. "Well, no. Not really. But we are going to hold a seance."

"I think that's a great idea," Tweed said grimly.

Because look how well it had turned out for Freddy and Marlene.

13 THE GHOSTS AND MR. SPEAKER

When Cheryl and Tweed poked their heads into the library, they weren't entirely surprised to see that it had been returned to a state of relative normalcy. Books were back on shelves, the goo was gone and only a faint whiff of eau-de-rotten-egg perfume lingered in the air. Even the grand piano was back in the middle of the black-and-white rug—all in one piece, not a key out of place!

"Huh," Cheryl whispered. "I was wondering what had happened to the wreckage ..."

"Weird," Tweed whispered back. "The house rebuilt it. Just like it rebuilt itself."

Cheryl tugged her by the sleeve across the hall into the dressing room and the others followed. She motioned for Tweed to hand over the speaker and turned it so the ruby eye was facing her. "You were a … a whaddayacallit back in the day, right?" Cheryl said to Simon. "A medium?"

"I always thought of myself as rather well-done!" the speaker answered and laughed at his own joke.

Cheryl rolled her eyes. "Look here, Speakie. There's something more to these ghosts than meets the eye. Er, what I mean by that is, we've never actually seen them. Only heard them. I don't think they're strong enough to appear to us. I think there is something preventing them from really showing up to the show. I wanna know what that something is." She turned to her cousin. "When we were in here before, I thought I saw—actually *saw*—them. Sort of. In those mirrors there."

Tweed kneeled down to examine the surface of the glass. "There are handprints—on the *inside*!"

"Exactly!" Cheryl nodded, leaning over her cousin's shoulder to examine the smudgy marks that had vanished earlier and had now reappeared. As if by … magic!

"You think they're—what—trapped in there?" Pilot asked. "Prisoners?"

"That's dastardly!" Artie exclaimed.

"Let's find out," Cheryl said. "Somebody go grab that crystal ball off the table in the library." She sank down cross-legged in the middle of the plush dressing-room carpet.

"I'll do it!" Feedback scurried off.

Cheryl told the others to join her in a circle on the floor and asked Tweed, who, between the two of them, was the film-based expert on the occult, to explain what they were about to do.

"A seance," Pilot said uneasily.

"Like in the movies."

"Yeah, but—"

"You said we needed monster-mashers, Flyboy." Artie snickered. "Be careful what you wish for!"

Pilot bit his tongue and let the twins do their thing.

"There are several different methodologies," Tweed said in a scholarly tone, "drawn from several different sources."

Cheryl nodded decisively as she attempted to fold her legs into the Lotus position. "Oh sure. You've got your straight-up general haunted house flicks—for example, our own expertly curated double bill—or you can go the more specialized seance-centric route with titles like just plain old *Seance!* or *Night of the Ghouls* or *Seance in Suite 777* ..."

"*The Trouble with Seances*." Tweed picked up the list. "*Ghost Host, The Crystal Ball Comrade*—a foreign film, obviously—*Hey, Spooky!* and *Hey, Spooky! 2: Electric Spookaloo, Host a Ghost*—"

"You already said *Host a Ghost*," Feedback pointed out, coming in with the crystal ball.

"I already said *Ghost Host*," Tweed corrected him.

"Oh."

Feedback blinked and handed the crystal ball down to Cheryl. The thing was as big as a fishbowl—the kind that could comfortably house a good-sized school of guppies—and surprisingly heavy, and she grunted with the effort of not dropping it as she placed it carefully on the floor in front of her.

"My point is, there are many variations on the procedure. But I think we should go for the straight-up classic," Tweed said with assurance. "Crystal ball, pad of paper for auto-writing in case any of us gets possessed, some questions, some answers, and hopefully nobody's eyeballs explode."

"Wait." Artie blinked rapidly. "Is that an actual possibility?"

Tweed shrugged. "Maybe keep yours closed. You're kind of susceptible to weird stuff like that."

Cheryl examined the crystal ball closely. It was large and heavy ... and hollow, with a hole in the bottom concealed by the elaborate brass stand on which it stood. It would have been easy for a sham mystic to pump a little dry ice fog in through that opening or shine a light up from a hole in the table on which it stood.

"Huh," Cheryl said and showed Tweed what she'd found.

"I'm thinking maybe our Mr. H wasn't *quite* as accomplished in the spectral arts as he professed to be," Tweed said, her eyes narrowing.

The disembodied voice of Simon Omar, ex-mystic, sighed from where Tweed had instructed Cheryl to place him on the floor in the middle of their circle. "Can't say as I blame the chap," he said. "I'll tell you, it wasn't easy. You really had to be a special kind of nutcase to commune with the spirit plane." His voice was instantly muffled when Cheryl suddenly plunked the oversized glass globe overtop of him like an astronaut's helmet. "I *was* that nutcase!"

"Good for you!" Cheryl enthused. "Be that nutcase again!"

"Right!"

Tweed told Pilot to cut the overhead lights and asked Feedback to light some of the candles that stood on the dressing-room vanity. When he couldn't find any matches, Feedback just shrugged and fired up the app on his phone that simulated a lighter flame and was useful for waving around at rock concerts during power ballads. Then, sitting in a circle on the floor, in the darkness and the silence, they waited.

"Okay ..." Tweed whispered. "Any time now ..."

"Psst." Cheryl nudged Simon's globe with her toe. "Make like a mystic."

"Hmm? Oh! Right ..." He hemmed. "Been a while. Let's see if I can remember how to do this now ... ah! I've got it. Hell*ooo* ... spirit plane?"

"Are you sure it *wasn't* just a malfunctioning stage prop that blew him up?" Pilot asked.

"Shh!" Tweed shushed him.

"Er, knock knock ..." The speaker tried again. "Anyone home?"

Silence.

"What's going on?" Artie asked, his eyes still squeezed shut behind his glasses. "My eyeballs aren't even tingling."

"*Shh!*" Cheryl shushed him.

The twins knew these things took time sometimes. It wasn't like just switching on a radio or—

Suddenly, they heard a sound like a switched-on radio coming from inside the crystal ball. A staticky sound, like the radio wasn't quite tuned to a station. Crackling and hissing and then a *weeeEEEOOoooOOWWwwee* noise filled the dressing room, as if an invisible hand was turning a dial trying to find a clear transmission.

Simon giggled and said, "Hey! That tickles!"

"Shh!" Tweed hushed him. "Concentrate."

The inside of the crystal ball began to glow crimson with the brightening light of the Spirit Stone and to fill with wispy, vaporous smoke. Simon cleared his throat— or, at least, made a sound like it—and stifled another giggle.

"I think I might be picking up something," he said, and his voice warbled strangely.

The misty wisps snaked out through the surface of the globe and into the room, slithering in serpentine fashion through the dark air, warping into grotesque faces and twisty, trailing limbs. Feedback's eyes were so wide Cheryl was afraid that, if anyone's eyeballs were going to explode, they'd be his, not Artie's. The digital flame on the screen of his phone suddenly began to flicker wildly.

Then it burst into a purple fireball and snuffed out, just like a real candle in a gust of wind.

"I think we've definitely attracted the attention of the spirit realm ..." Simon said nervously.

Even without the phone light, there was enough pulsing crimson illumination in the room, coming from the crystal ball and its occupant, to confirm that Simon's assessment was a little on the conservative side. Attracted the spirit realm's attention? More like, invited them to a fancy-dress party!

The twins and their friends watched in astonishment as the vaporous entities floating about the room suddenly went for the racks of clothes and began to tug at them. A couple of the lace and satin dresses slipped from the hangers and began to swirl and float about the room like a pair of dancers at a ball, graceful and terrifying at the same time.

"Former occupants of the house, I think," Simon murmured. "Having a bit of fun ..."

Unable to resist peeking at what was happening, Artie had popped open one eye in time to see an identical suit to the one he was wearing jerk from its hanger like a puppet on strings. It flapped about awkwardly as a head on a long skinny neck and gangly limbs poked out of the collar and cuffs. The head bore the beaky-nosed face of an old man who peered through beady, angry eyes at the excessive lengths of wrist and ankle he was showing.

"Who shrunk my suit?" he demanded in a warbly voice. It would have been pretty hilarious if it wasn't quite so terrifying. Then he peered about the room. "Who are you gaggle of urchins?" he asked in an accusing screech. "What do ye here?"

"Uh … we … we're …" Cheryl stammered, her heart in her throat as the ghost's eyes blazed red.

"Art thou on my lawn?!" the creepy old ghost shrieked, clearly unhinged at the prospect. "Avaunt and quit my yard!"

His whole head was blazing now, like a jack-o'-lantern carved by an overly enthusiastic trick-or-treater, and the dancing dresses were gyrating and throwing their sleeves in the air in dismay.

The circle of friends sent up a collective wail of terror …

And *POOF!*

The suit and dresses dropped limply to the floor.

All was suddenly silent. And dim. Only a faint glow pulsed from Simon's Spirit Stone inside the globe. There was the faint scratching of a pencil on paper and they all turned to see Artie scribbling away.

"Art-Bart?" Pilot asked warily. "Are you possessed?"

"What?" Artie blinked his one open eye and looked down at the notepad. "Oh. No. I doodle when I'm terrified. See?" He held it up. "Snoopy."

Everyone breathed a sigh of relief, except Cheryl, who rounded on the crystal ball. "What didja do that for?!" she demanded angrily. "Who in the heck was that old geezer?"

"Don't ask me!" Simon protested. "I just opened the portal! I can't control who comes through—"

"That was Granddad Hecklestone. He was a big old meanie."

"Oh," Cheryl said. "Well, that explains—GAH! Who said that?!"

They all turned toward where the whispery voice had come from, and there, standing—well, *floating*, really—in each of the dressing room's three long mirrors, were the shades of the Hecklestone children fading into view: Daphne, Roderick and Edwina.

"I'ma gedoutta here," Feedback squeaked. "*Please?*"

"Please ..." echoed one of the shadows in a polite and very proper English accent. "Don't leave us. We didn't mean to frighten you ..."

"Guh ... g-guh ..." Artie began to stammer. "Guh-g-guh ..."

"Ghosts," Pilot finished for him in a strained whisper. "Yeah. I think we've established that."

"Holy moly," Cheryl said.

"*Cooool ...*" Tweed said. "Also, incredibly terrifying."

"The Hecklestone kids, I presume?" Pilot said, and swallowed nervously.

The tallest apparition—a willowy young girl who looked to be about ten years old, with ringlets tied up in bows and a pretty lace dress with a high collar—nodded.

"You must be Daphne," Pilot said cautiously and tipped his hat to her.

The girl curtsied prettily. "My siblings, Roderick and Edwina."

Edwina, who looked to be about seven, floated off to the side of her mirror so that she peeked out shyly around the frame, her pinkie finger stuck in the side of her mouth. Roderick, who was dressed in yet another dapper little suit almost identical to Artie's borrowed duds, gave a little gentlemanly bow. He was tall for his age whereas Artie was short for his, which had worked out nicely in Artie's favour, tailoring-wise.

"What are you doing in there?" Artie asked.

"We're grounded," Roderick said with a sour pout.

"The house ..." Edwina said in a shy whisper. "It's very angry with us."

"Your friend in the metal box was right," Daphne explained. "After so many years of our father holding his seances and conducting his experiments, this house is more ectoplasm than brick and plaster!"

"Why's it angry?" Tweed asked.

"Because we exploded it up!" Roderick exclaimed and floated in a twirl inside his mirror with his arms outstretched, making explosion noises.

Daphne rolled her ghostly eyes in the direction of her little brother's mirror. "We didn't mean to. But now it's punishing us. It won't let us go. It's making us do things—mean things—to you."

"Naughty house!" Edwina made a terribly fierce little scowl.

"We just want to be free," Daphne said. "We want to leave."

"Er ... I don't know if that's exactly possible," Simon muttered.

"Then maybe *you* could all stay!" Edwina said. "It *has* been fun having someone else to play with again."

"Play with?!" Cheryl sputtered. "What the—you mean like when you threw a piano at us! I heard you little brats laughing. You coulda killed us, you know!"

"The house made us do it—I swear!" Daphne pleaded.

"It really did." Roderick nodded. "But it *was* a spectacular crash! Even if it was only an illusion. We used to do things like that all the time with our governesses." He grinned. "They never minded. Of course, most never seemed to last for very long ..."

"Well, listen here!" Tweed said sternly. "We're your babysitters—"

"Our what?" Edwina asked.

"Your ... er ... governators!" Cheryl clarified. "And there'll be no more of that kind of behaviour tonight!"

Edwina pouted. "Boo."

"That's what all the ghosts say," Tweed said.

"What happened the night the house went kablooie?" Feedback asked. "What caused the explosion?"

"That was all Roderick's fault!" Edwina said, jamming her chubby fists on her ghostly hips and glaring at her departed brother.

"Was not!" Roderick said and reached out the side of his mirror, into Edwina's, and yanked on one of her pale braids.

"Ow! Was too!"

The two ghostlings started a spectral slap fight that was pretty strange to watch, because their hands kept passing through each other.

"Hey," Tweed said. *"Hey!"*

They turned to her.

"Now cut that out," she admonished. "Like Cheryl said. We're the sitters here and so you have to do what we say. Now. Tell us what happened."

"Daddy was away—again—and Daphne and I were bored," Edwina said.

"The latest governess had handed in her resignation— after a whole week this time," Daphne explained, "and the domestic agency told us there was no one to replace her on short notice so we'd have to fend for ourselves that night. Imagine."

"Imagine." Artie snorted. "No one to torment!"

"Exactly!" Daphne exclaimed, as if it made perfect sense. "Such a bore. So Eddy and I thought, for a lark, that we'd try to contact Mumsy in the beyond."

"Daddy was forever holding seances," Edwina piped

up. "And I always listened at the keyhole. So we knew how to go about it. But Roddy's a silly old boy and didn't want to play. He went off tinkering in the silly old basement instead."

"Which was *strictly* not allowed!" Daphne shook a ghost finger at her little ghost brother but he just stuck his ghost tongue out at her. "Daddy kept all the dangerous toys in there locked up tight."

"You found the trap door, didn't you?" Tweed asked.

"Yup!" Roderick nodded brightly. "Daddy would use it to make ghosts appear sometimes when the seances he held weren't going so well. Old magician's trick."

"Ha!" Simon barked a muffled laugh from inside his globe. "Told you so. Old Heck was a faker!"

"Only sometimes," Daphne said. "But he had to keep up appearances so that all his tea-and-seance ladies would keep coming back."

Cheryl shook her head at the mischief-makers. "So you two holed up in the study messing around with stuff you shouldn't have—"

"How were we supposed to know it would *actually* work?" Edwina pouted.

"—and *you* went down into the lab and started messing around with stuff you shouldn't have—"

Roderick shrugged innocently. "How was I supposed to know nitroglycerin was *that* explosive?"

"Right. And so *your* little chemistry experiment," Cheryl continued, "and *your* inter-dimensional tea party combined to send this old house ka-booming right into the stratosphere."

"Sadly." Daphne nodded. "Then, as far as I can tell from what you've all been saying about those carnival shenanigans and such, *you* lot messed around with matters you shouldn't have and look where we all are now!"

"Touché," Cheryl admitted. It had, after all, been their rescue of Zahara-Safiya that had started the whole ball of mystical wax rolling.

"It's a *naughty* house!" Edwina pouted and kicked the surface of her mirror. The image in the glass rippled outward from where she'd made contact.

"So what's the deal with this whole house-sitter competition?" Feedback asked.

"Well, when the house rebuilt itself—with us poor shades trapped inside, subject to its *awfully* grumpy will—and we regained awareness of all that had happened, Roddy and Eddy and I became desperate," Daphne explained. "We thought we'd try and possess some of the local townsfolk and try to escape."

"You were gonna *possess* us?!" Tweed glared disapprovingly at the trio.

"Not you. Them. The two girls that left. And, well, you." Daphne pointed at Feedback.

"Not cool!" Feedback exclaimed, going pale at the thought. "*Not* cool!"

"If you only wanted Cindy and Hazel and Karl"— Pilot frowned—"then why did you invite C and T, here?"

"We didn't." Daphne shrugged.

"Here we go again!" Cheryl threw her hands up in the air. "What the heck's wrong with us? Is it this thirteen thing again? Is that it?"

"Well." Daphne shrugged. "You *are* twelve."

"ARRGH!" Cheryl's pigtails bounced in her frustration.

"It's only that, without a governess, if we managed to successfully possess someone, we'd have to fend for ourselves," Daphne explained. "And thirteen is a more respectable age to be out and about in the world. We could get nice jobs."

"Or go to the pubs!" Roderick clapped his hands.

"Er … maybe back in Victorian days you could," Pilot said. "But not now. And I don't think most of the jobs back then were very nice."

"Well, it's rather beside the point now." Daphne sighed. "Those other girls turned out to be quite selfish and, while very competent at complaining and picking locks and eating sweeties, rather useless overall. Not at all capable of helping us out the way you lot seem to be. No imagination! That's why we siphoned some of the ectoplasm out of the door lock and helped them escape when the house was distracted by you having a bash at the windows."

"Told you," Simon said.

"Well, I guess that explains that," Tweed said,

allowing herself a slightly satisfied grin. "What it doesn't explain is why we got the invites anyway."

"Er ... Mrowr ..." From beneath a hanging rack of frilly petticoats, the gargoyle Ramshackle made a slightly guilty noise.

"*You* did that, Shack?" Artie asked.

"Murmmle-rrorwrgg," the gargoyle answered. "Mrowow."

"Uh-huh ..."

The gargoyle chirped and burbled away, Artie nodding as he listened.

"Uh-huh ..."

"What's he saying, Shrimpcake?" Cheryl asked impatiently.

Artie put up a finger and listened some more. "Uh-huh ... right." He turned to the others. "He said the Hecksters, here, sent him out to find three suitable possession candidates to lure to the house after dusk yesterday. He found Cindy and Hazel gossiping about sitter stuff in the park—something about the latest Binky Barker episode and how Hazel had managed to set her free—and figured they'd do for the girls. Then Feedback's name came up and Shack thought he was good to go. He waited around, resting his damaged wing in a tree, until he could follow Cindy and Hazel home. And that's when he heard them saying stuff about *you* two. After he delivered the invites, he kinda had second thoughts. Ramshackle thinks weirdness is an *asset*, y'see. So, he dropped off another invitation at the barn."

"Huh. At least someone around here recognizes our superiorness-ness." Cheryl flipped a pigtail over her ear and squared her shoulders. "Right. So I guess this is where we get on with the mission, then."

"What?! *What* mission?" Feedback sputtered. "Are you seriously considering helping set these three loony spooks loose on an unsuspecting Wiggins?"

The twins exchanged a glance with Artie and Pilot. *Well? Were they?*

"Uh … yeah," Tweed said after a moment.

"Yup." Pilot nodded.

"Heck yes!" Artie enthused, always up for a healthy dose of looniness.

"Look …" Cheryl explained. "It's okay if you don't want in on this. That's cool. But … last time we met somebody we thought was a dangerous, supernaturally souped-up evil nutcase, it turned out she was just a lonely kid looking for a bit of help."

"I …" Feedback blinked, frowning. "I …"

"Attaboy, Feedback!" Cheryl clapped him on the shoulder and turned briskly back to the matter at hand, as did the others.

"How'd Ramshackle find our barn?" Tweed wondered.

"Guys." Pilot rolled his eyes. "You've put flyers on

pretty much every power pole and mailbox in the whole town. Couldn't have been too hard—"

"BUT I DON'T WANNA BE POSSESSED!" Feedback suddenly blurted at the top of his lungs.

In the silence that followed, everyone turned to look at him.

"I mean ..." he continued, red-faced, "okay. I'll help. But a guy's gotta draw the line somewhere."

Cheryl had to stifle a snort of amusement and Tweed bit her lip.

Artie just rolled his eyes. "Don't be such a baby. It's nuthin'."

"And you don't need to worry about it now anyway," Roderick said sourly. "It turns out we don't actually know *how* to possess people. This ghostly business is really rather harder than it looks." He nodded at Artie. "I tried and was *almost* able to possess that one when he was standing there in my suit, in front of my mirror. It didn't work. Instead, I think I just managed to class the chap up a bit."

"Hey! *You* stole my clothes!" Artie exclaimed.

"I gave you dapper new ones!"

"And you threw this book at me!"Artie brandished the tome. "And that was definitely *not* any old piano-pushing illusion! That hurt! D'you know how heavy this thing is? You coulda broke my schnozz!" He pointed to his still slightly pink nose.

Roderick blinked. "I didn't do that. I mean— bravo!—but it wasn't me."

"One of you sure as heck did." Artie glared at the mirrors accusingly.

"Mrwr."

"Ramshackle?!" He turned to gape at the mini-monster, whose mini-monstrous face bore a somewhat sheepish look. "I thought we were pals," Artie said in a hurt tone. "What didja do *that* for?"

The little monster huffed and furrowed his horned brow. As much as it seemed that the gargoyle and Artie shared a certain kind of rapport, it was clear that, judging from the expression on Ramshackle's face, there was only so much information he could coherently convey to his human buddy through his repertoire of gurgles and growls. Kind of like, if you knew how to speak Cat, you could *talk* to a cat. But you couldn't necessarily have a deep and meaningful philosophical argument or a discussion on how to rebuild the carburetor on a 1964 Mercury Comet. Still, Ramshackle was clearly trying to make a point. He flapped a little ways into the air, snatched the book with his front paws and reared back. It looked like he was going to go for Artie's head again.

"*Whoa* there, little fella!" Cheryl lunged and plucked the book from the gargoyle's grasp before he could lob the thing.

"I think he's trying to tell us something," Tweed said.

Ramshackle turned and gave her a distinctly "ya *think*?" expression.

"Here," she said to Cheryl. "Hand me the book."

Cheryl handed over the antique volume and Tweed flipped it around so that they could all see the lettering on the ornately embossed leather of the front cover. The ghost kids in the mirror crowded against the glass and Ramshackle made excited purring noises of encouragement as Tweed read the title out loud.

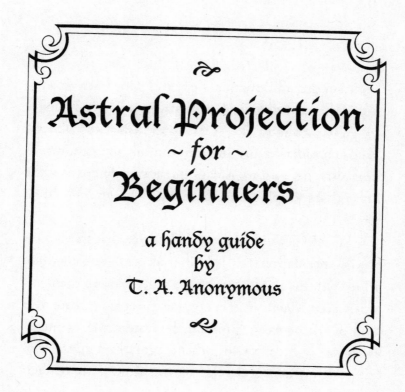

Astral Projection
~ for ~
Beginners

a handy guide
by
T. A. Anonymous

14 THE REALLY GREAT ESCAPE

"I don't get it," Artie said.

"I do," Tweed said. "Ramshackle was trying to help."

"What, exactly, was he trying to help with?" Cheryl asked, considering the matter with all due caution. "I mean, isn't he, y'know, *part* of the house? And isn't it the house that's keeping our charming threesome in thrall, here?"

"I think," Tweed mused, "and I agree that this is a bit of wild speculation, but I think it *might* have something to do with his wing. Maybe the chip is more than just superficial. Maybe the energy surge actually caused a kind of rift between him and the house itself. I mean, when we got here, we saw other gargoyles up on the roof but none of them seem to have taken on a life of their own ..."

"I remember when the little stone bat-kitty got hurt," Edwina said. "It was the night Mumsy got the zap! Bat-kitty got the zap, too! Naughty storm."

Cheryl shivered at the casual way the little girl mentioned the lightning strike that had resulted in the untimely demise of her mother but, she supposed, when you're a ghost yourself, maybe stuff like that didn't bother you quite so much.

"See?" Artie said. "I was right! He *did* get hit by lightning."

"Mrrf." Ramshackle screwed up his face in distaste and ruffled his ragged wing.

"Okay," Pilot said. "So we're sure the little dude's definitely playing on the right ball team. What's his pitch?"

Tweed flipped open the book and they all crowded around. There was a flowery chapter of introduction, describing the wonders of the spirit plane and how the author had magically unlocked the mysteries of how to not only *get* there, but navigate one's way *back* again. Entire sections were devoted to what sounded like a bunch of New-Agey go-with-the-flow mystical stuff. But then there was page after page of diagrams with strange mechanical and mathematical notations. On one of them, there was a star and arrows and handwritten notations in the margins, scribbled there in pencil that was almost too faded to read. It was a page that displayed detailed instructions on how to build a device that, once activated, would super-boost your average, sparkly floaty spectral signal and focus it like a laser beam.

Frankly, it all sounded like a whole lotta hocus-pocus mumbo-jumbo techno-babble to Cheryl and Tweed. Feedback and Pilot, however, both got the same kind of gleam in their eyes as they flipped through the schematics. Mechanics and gadgets sang a siren song to the two boys.

"T. A. *Anonymous*." Simon chortled to himself, casting his ruby eye beam on the book. "I'll bet dollars to doorknobs—even mystically infused ones—that book was written by Thomas Alva Edison, the old Wizard of Menlo Park, himself. Attaboy, Tommy!"

"Gimme the cheat notes version," Artie said. "What does it say?"

"The book says, basically," Feedback summarized, "that astral projection and spectral manifestation are not only possible, they're kinda a breeze. It's all about … er, hmm …"—he ran his finger along the sentences on a page—"a 'strong emotional connection supported and enhanced by the latest in modern technology.' All you need to power the machine is an energy source, and a … the author calls it a 'lodestone.' A 'physical object replete with emotional resonance strong enough to act as a homing beacon.' That's the catch. Having a strong enough connection to *this* plane to be able to come back to it."

Tweed beckoned Cheryl over into a corner of the

dressing room, away from the mirror where the Hecklestone kids still floated, waiting patiently to be set free of their ectoplasmic constraints (*mostly* patiently— Roderick looked like he might be starting to fashion a tiny slingshot out of a shoelace and a tie clip). "We have a problem," Tweed whispered. "The only connection the Heck kids have is to *this* place. Even if we figure out a way to build this thing so we can leave, they couldn't. They'd just wind up right back here."

"We can take them with us," Cheryl whispered back.

"Where?"

"Uh … C+T headquarters?" Cheryl shrugged helplessly. "The Moviemobile? The mini-golf range?"

"Any of those would do, I guess," Tweed said. "Except we'd need something to use as a lodestone."

The twins thought about that. Tweed had Nerf darts (and garlic powder) from headquarters and Cheryl had her putter, but neither of those things seemed to have the kind of heartfelt oomph needed for both girls to ensure they could pull everyone along with them.

"We don't have anything like that," Artie was saying.

"Like *heck* we don't!" Pilot said triumphantly. "Like heck *you* don't!"

The twins turned to gape at their best friend, wondering what on earth—or the earthly plane, exactly—he could possibly be talking about.

"Never mind astral projection," he said, excitedly. "What about an astral projec*tor*? The one back at the

Starlight Paradise? You need an object? Something with powerful emotional—whaddayacallit—resonance?" He turned to address the others in the room, the Heck kids included, and pointed a finger at the girls. "Well, I don't know *anything* that's got a stronger bond than the one between the Drive-In and these two girls, except maybe me and my plane. Now I don't have a piece of my plane handy, but I've got this!" Pilot reached into the pocket of his overalls and pulled out a piece of silver metal blackened on one end.

He held it aloft like a beacon of hope.

A befuddled silence fell on the room.

Artie cleared his throat and said, "And that thing … *is?*"

Pilot rolled his eyes. "It's a tungsten electrode from the xenon bulb that was in the Drive-In 3D movie projector that got hit by lightning during that storm a while back!" he explained, as if it was the most obvious thing in the world. "Pops and I did the repairs on it earlier today and I put this in my pocket and forgot about it. He's running that very same projector tonight because your double bill was over capacity yesterday." He checked his watch. "We've been here long enough that they're probably halfway through the second feature by now!"

"Ding Dong, You're Dead!" Cheryl exclaimed. She and Tweed beamed at each other. Even in the midst of a paranormal crisis, the girls were proud of their programming success. "It's perfect!"

"But …" Tweed frowned, momentarily unsure. She nodded her head in the direction of the mirrors and whispered to Cheryl, "What if we pull *them* out of this place with us and they … you know … stay ghosts?"

"It doesn't matter," Daphne said, having overheard them in spite of the whispering. "Either way, we'll be free to move on. We won't be trapped anymore. That's all we want—however it turns out."

"And maybe a bang-up, good old-fashioned explosion to send us on our way!" Roderick enthused.

Edwina just nodded in placid agreement with her sister and brother.

"Whaddaya think, Mr. Omar?" Feedback asked the speaker. "Could we use something like that electro-thingy in the book to get home?"

Simon harrumphed. "Why are you asking me?"

Feedback shrugged. "You *are* the resident expert on—"

"On blowing myself to smithereens!" Simon protested. "Or have you pack of marauding ragamuffins forgotten that?"

"Yeah, but," Cheryl said, "you'll be better at it this time. Practice and all. And you have us to help you. And the book!" She stabbed at the diagram on the page with a freckled finger. "I mean *look* at these diagrams. The ones with the pencil scribbles beside them! There's a whole basement full of gadgets and gears just like this stuff. I even saw a half-built something-or-other under a sheet that looked almost identical to Figures 6-a through 7-c right here on page 42. Only … it might've been missing some key bits and pieces here and there …"

"Are you saying that Hector Hecklestone already tried to build one of these things?" Tweed asked.

"Maybe." Cheryl shrugged. "Could be he was trying every way possible to get in touch with the dearly departed missus, and just didn't get the chance to finish the gadget before the house went BOOM. And if that's the case, then all *we* have to do is, y'know, add some bits and tighten some bolts, get Old Heck's focusy-whatchamy-thingy up and chugging and Bob's your uncle!"

And that's when the enthusiasm for the project ground to a screeching halt.

Pilot and Feedback exchanged a glance.

"Who are we kidding?" Feedback said, staring down at the complicated spiderweb lines of the mechanical schematics. "We could *never* finish building a thing like this by ourselves. We're kids."

"Yeah …" Pilot nodded reluctantly. "This is way out of our league."

"Bite your tongue, Yeager Armbruster!" Cheryl said. "And you too, Karl!"

"Yeah," Tweed agreed in a fierce, determined monotone. "You want *league*? *We're* the League of Awesome!"

"Yes!" Cheryl enthused. And then, "No!"

"What?" Tweed blinked at her.

There was a gleam in Cheryl's eye as she said, "No … I don't think the superhero scenario is quite going to cut it on this one …"

"Well, what then?" Tweed leaned forward in anticipation of what her feisty cousin had come up with. "What should we do?"

"What does anyone do in a movie when they have to accomplish a seemingly impossible task in a limited amount of time?" Cheryl asked. "You know, something big like … like building a barn in a day. Or learning smokin' moves in time for the big dance. Or getting totally pumped up before the heavyweight champion title fight!"

Tweed clenched her fists, ready for a challenge. "You mean …"

"I do." Cheryl nodded seriously. "Heckle-dude had a book and he had a blowtorch. But *we* have what *he* didn't: one handy-dandy powerful mystic-in-a-speaker-in-a-jar, three ghosts-with-the-mosts, a mythical magical house pet with wings and a whole houseful of ecto-magic just waiting to be tapped for that little extra whammy we might need to get the job done. Plus we have the guts, we have the grit, we have the gumption." She paused for dramatic effect. "Only *one* thing stands in our way."

"I know." Tweed furrowed her brow and slapped her fist into her palm in frustration. They were *so* close. "If *only* we had some '80s music."

"Uh ..." Feedback lifted his hand. "I got that."

Artie blinked at him. "You do?"

"Sure." He brandished his phone. "I gotta whole playlist of that stuff."

The others crowded around as Feedback's fingers zigged and zagged over the little glowy screen of his smartphone, calling up a list of power ballads and synth-heavy, soft-rock croon tunes and drum-machine-driven pop-rock anthems.

It was perfect.

The twins high-fived triumphantly.

"Looks like we've got ourselves the ingredients for an '80s-style movie montage sequence that'll bring the house down!" Cheryl crowed. "Literally!"

"Shrimpcake!" Tweed exclaimed. "Bring that book over here!"

"Pilot!" Cheryl called. "Get that monkey wrench up to speed!"

"Feedback! Get ready to hit Play!"

The boys jumped to do the girls' bidding, caught up in their infectious enthusiasm. Ramshackle took to the air above their heads, swooping and diving in excited, if somewhat erratic, loop-de-loops.

The air in the room crackled with anticipation.

This, the twins knew, might very well prove to be their most challenging bout of ACTION!! to date. It would take fierce concentration, razor-sharp precision, laser-like focus, cracker-jack timing, guts, grit, luck, skill and a healthy dose of imagination overdrive.

The twins exchanged their C+T Secret Signal (patent pending)—not *quite* so secret now, as the others joined in—and gave the order.

"Cameras rolling …"

"Aaaaand …"

"... ACTION!!"

INT. THE STATELY DINING ROOM OF A HAUNTED MANSION, CIRCA 1983 -- NIGHT

CAMERA CLOSE-UP on a LARGE, LEATHER-BOUND BOOK. A hand flips the book open and the pages begin to flip, faster and faster ... and then, stop! The hand points to a diagram on a page.

> OFF-CAMERA VOICE
> Eureka. That's it. Let's get to work.

SFX: '80s POP-ROCK MUSIC WITH A DRIVING BEAT STARTS UP, PLAYS THROUGHOUT. This is the classic '80s-STYLE MOVIE MONTAGE SEQUENCE.

CAMERA ROTATES IN A 360° SWEEP TO REVEAL A FIERCELY DETERMINED RAGTAG AGAINST-ALL-ODDS TEAM OF '80s MISFIT KIDS ON A MISSION TO BUILD AN ASTRAL PROJECTOR AND SAVE THE DAY. CAMERA PANS over each member of the TEAM. First, the REBELLIOUS GOTH KID, in HEAVY EYELINER:

> GOTH KID
> I'll put the coffee on.

THE SCRAPPY KID, wearing a HEADBAND, OFF-SHOULDER SWEATSHIRT AND LEG WARMERS:

> SCRAPPY KID
> I'll clear some work space!

THE BRAINY KID, dressed in a MICHAEL JACKSON
THRILLER-ERA JACKET:

                    BRAINY KID
          I'll start on the equations!

THE OVERALLS KID, dressed in, er, OVERALLS
(ACID-WASH, ONE STRAP UNDONE):

                   OVERALLS KID
          I'll do something useful with this
          wrench!

THE SHRIMPY KID, inexplicably dressed in
HEAVY SWEATS AND KNIT CAP WITH A TOWEL AROUND
HIS NECK:

                   SHRIMPY KID
          I'll get started on the skipping rope
          and punching bag!

236

THE KIDS SCATTER! OVERLAPPING JUMP-CUT
SEQUENCE of SHOTS:

SCRAPPY KID yanks a tablecloth -- magician-
style -- out from under a dozen place-
settings and tall candelabras on a long table
(unsuccessfully). The awesome '80s music
is momentarily drowned out by the CRASH OF
BREAKING CROCKERY!!

In the background, SHRIMPY KID WORKS THE JUMP
ROPE.

                                        CUT TO:

GOTH KID maniacally brews coffee using MAD-
SCIENTIST LAB EQUIPMENT.

In the background, SHRIMPY KID WORKS THE
PUNCHING BAG.

                                        CUT TO:

BRAINY KID fills a CHALKBOARD with INSANELY
COMPLICATED EQUATIONS.

In the background, SHRIMPY KID GOES A FEW
ROUNDS WITH A SIDE OF BEEF.

                                        CUT TO:

OVERALLS KID hauls on a ROPE-AND-PULLEY
SYSTEM attached to HEAVY MACHINERY.

In the background, SHRIMPY KID LIES FLAT ON
HIS BACK IN THE MIDDLE OF A BOXING RING WITH
ANIMATED "TWEETY-BIRD" GARGOYLES CIRCLING HIS
HEAD.

                                        CUT TO:

WIDE SHOT of the room. It is ORGANIZED
CHAOS!! BRAINY SCRIBBLES MADLY, GOTHY AND
OVERALLS TINKER FRANTICALLY, SCRAPPY RUN/
DANCES CRAZILY ON THE SPOT, SHRIMPY DOES ONE-
ARM PUSH-UPS ...

                                        CUT TO:

EXTREME CAMERA CLOSE-UP on a PLASMA GLOBE,
CRACKLING WITH TENDRILS OF ENERGY.

                                        CUT TO:

LONG, HIGH-ANGLE SHOT OF THE TEAM, THE
MIRACULOUS MACHINE -- A CRAZILY EMBELLISHED
FILM-PROJECTOR-LIKE CONTRAPTION SURROUNDED
BY A CIRCLE OF PLASMA GLOBES, CONNECTED BY
WIRES, AND FOCUSED ON THREE TALL STANDING
MIRRORS.

IT IS MAGNIFICENT IN ITS IMPOSSIBLENESS.

                                    CUT TO:

THE TEAM STANDS, ADMIRING THEIR
ACCOMPLISHMENT.

                    SCRAPPY KID
                (fiercely satisfied)
        Eureeeka.

CAMERA CRANES UP as THE TEAM, in a circle,
THROW THEIR ARMS IN THE AIR TRIUMPHANTLY!!

                    THE TEAM
                   (in unison)
            HECKLESTOOOONNNE!!

    FADE OUT AS THE MUSIC DRIFTS TO SILENCE ...

"CUT!! ..."

"Aaaaaand ... cut," Tweed said with quiet satisfaction.

"Cut, indeed." Cheryl nodded, arms crossed over her chest.

"Wow," Feedback whispered into the silence following the frenzied activity of the ACTION!! sequence. "That almost felt like we *were* possessed ..."

"The magic of the movies, pal." Pilot grinned and clapped him on the shoulder.

"I can't believe it." Simon the mystic speaker's voice was hushed in awe.

"You *better* believe it." Tweed wiped her brow with the sleeve of her jacket.

"Yeah!" Cheryl tugged her pigtails straight. "*That's* the most important part!"

"You did it," Simon said. "You *really* did it. *We* did it! It's done. Huzzah! Bravo. Yadda yadda. Now could someone *please* take this fishbowl off my head? I'm suffocating here!"

"You know you don't actually have lungs anymore, right?" Pilot said, lifting the globe off and setting it aside.

The speaker made a gasping sound nonetheless.

Cheryl picked Simon up and tucked him under her arm, and together the team turned to survey the Machine of Awesome. It was like a cross between the inside of a madman's projection booth and Dr. Frankenstein's laboratory, criss-crossed with wires linking up all sorts of precariously cobbled-together cogs and wheels and gears and electrodes and ... and ... *things*. Pilot and Feedback had done an admirable job of at least making the thing look like it did in the pictures. It actually hadn't proved that hard, if only because pretty much all of the widgets and whatnots in Sir Hecklestone's basement had been manufactured at roughly the same time period as the book was written.

The Astral Projector stood at one end of the long dining room and the dressing-room mirrors, which had been brought downstairs, now stood at the other. They had decided to give their creation that particular name to correspond nicely with the Starlight projector. And once Simon Omar had pointed out that the words *astral* and *star* meant pretty much the same thing, well, of course, that just convinced the whole crew that they were really onto something with this whole crazy idea. Surrounding the projector in a half-circle, the plasma balls were wired up and flickering away, their dancing miniature streaks of lightning mimicked by distant flashes through the tall windows. A storm was coming.

Cheryl checked her watch. "Holy moly—it's almost pushin' midnight! The second movie on the bill should be almost over by now. I sure hope the Drive-In doesn't get rained out on the last reel!" she worried, her priorities, as always, firmly in check.

Pilot did some last-minute tinkering with the giant ON/OFF lever-switch box he'd bolted onto the end of the long dining-room table, attached to the projector by a length of coloured cables. Then he checked the placement of the Drive-In's burnt-out tungsten filament. Feedback fiddled with the focus lens. Artie, for his part, just paced back and forth in front of the Hecklestone kids in their mirrors, giving pep talks like a pre-game coach. Finally, Cheryl and Tweed realized that everyone was pretty much just stalling.

"Okay, okay," Cheryl said, setting Simon down on the table, pointing at the mirrors. "Let's get this show on the astral road. I mean ... uh ..." She cleared her throat and enunciated precisely, and with grand gesturing. "Ladies and Gentlemen, shall we?"

"Mr. Omar?" Tweed said formally. "If you would please do the honours and initiate contact with the astral plane in preparation for our takeoff and travel?"

Really, they were all just winging it, procedure-wise, but they figured the more structured and, well, Victorian they could make things, the better. Put on a good show and all that. Even the Heck kids had all ghost-morphed into what looked like their Sunday best.

"Delighted to, oh lovely and talented assistants," Simon said graciously.

"Assistants ...?" Cheryl muttered, but let it slide, under the circumstances.

The air in the room began to shudder and Simon's jewel illuminated the end of the room with a bright, crimson light. For a long moment, nothing seemed to be happening. Then the air grew misty.

"I hope Grandpa Ghost doesn't put in an appearance again," Artie muttered.

"Pilot," Tweed said in a calm, quiet voice, "I think it's time. Hit it."

Pilot reached over to the big lever on the table and—with a noise like KA-CHUNKK!!—threw the switch. Then he stepped quickly out of the way as the projector chugged its way up to speed. A kind of dancing, sparkling, green-and-gold light raced out in a widening beam and washed over the surface of the mirrors. Edwina giggled and squirmed like she was being tickled and Roddy spun in circles, while Daphne just bounced up and down a bit and grinned.

Cheryl and Tweed beamed almost as brightly as the projector, both of them sighing the same blissful, happy sigh they felt every single time they settled in to watch a picture. Only, this time, they weren't just watching it. They were about to become a part of it. And Pilot was absolutely right: the projector was the girls' bond with the Drive-In that would carry them all safely home.

The three mirrors, side by side, seemed to merge into one seamless, wavering picture, and Daphne, Roderick and Edwina smiled broadly and stepped closer to link hands. In the dim background behind the Hecklestone trio, figures and sets started to appear. The twins instantly recognized their old friends from the attic scene in *Ding Dong, You're Dead*, preparing for the climactic seance scene. Only, it was like they were watching it from behind the screen! All the images were reversed.

"Remember what we talked about," Tweed said. "Whatever happens, whoever gets through, just keep on running. Head for the big red barn and hide out there until we can regroup."

Cheryl nodded, tense and ready for action, one hand stretched out so she could grab the Drive-In speaker when the moment came. Together, C+T and Co. prepared to make a charging run for the wavering surface of the mirror, where they would grab the Hecklestone kids, hold tight and keep on running. But, suddenly, the illumination from the Astral Projector and Simon's Spirit Stone seemed to wash out beneath a lurid ghoulish-green glare that spilled in through the wide-open doors that led to the grand foyer. There was the sound of furious flapping followed by a noise like the squawking of an outraged rooster fighting with a barn cat, and Artie abruptly left his post by the mirrors.

"Ramshackle!" he cried out as he sprinted down the length of the room.

"Artie!"

"Art-Bart!"

"Shrimpcake!"

Tweed, Pilot and Cheryl ran after him. Out in the foyer, they saw that the big bronze doorknob was glowing with fury. The house seemed to have finally clued in to what they were trying to do and was either sending out a beam of fiery green ectoplasm *into* their machine to try to short it, or it was sucking the ectoplasmic fire *out* of their machine to try to drain it. It was hard to tell. Either way, it was a BAD THING.

And Ramshackle was caught right in the middle of it.

It looked as though the little guy had thrown himself in harm's way to try to deflect the house's wrath and now he was caught in it. Tiny forks of blue-white lightning danced crazily along his outstretched wings like he was trying to fight back.

"Guys!" Feedback called frantically from the dining room. "GUYS!! We're losing power! The plasma globes are firing erratically and the portal is fading! We need more juice or we're not gonna make it!"

The Hecklestone children began to wail in panic. The house began to roar with rage. Thunder boomed outside and lightning crashed and flashed. The windows began to rattle like ... well, like regular windows.

And Cheryl had an idea.

"Tweed!" she shouted. "Catch!" She drew her trusty mini-golf putter—without the tattered rubber grip it was really just an old metal rod—and threw it to her cousin, who caught it deftly out of the air with one hand. "Give it to Ramshackle!"

Then she seized the fireplace poker she'd left lying in the entryway earlier and, while the house was otherwise occupied with more important business, managed to smash one windowpane to smithereens. Only a small one but that was the best she could do. Cheryl had seen in a movie that folks who were hit by lightning once were more likely to be hit by lightning again. She didn't know if that was true or not, but she thought it was worth a try. And Ramshackle was kind of made of magic anyway.

Tweed thought she knew what Cheryl was trying to do, and when she thrust the skinny metal club into the gargoyle's reaching paw, she saw in his glowy little eyes that he did, too. For a moment, nothing happened. Then Ramshackle roared a roar of defiance and held the putter aloft. A blinding streak of lightning forked through the shattered window and arrowed straight for the putter!

"Shack!" Artie screamed.

A fireworks-bright explosion of sparks lit up the room. When it dimmed, the twins and their friends looked up to see another ghostly figure, hovering in the air above the flapping gargoyle and outlined with the same flickering lightning flickers.

"Mumsy!" the three Hecks cried delightedly.

The regal, shadowy figure turned and smiled at them. "Hello, darlings," she said in an echoey voice. "Behaving nicely for your minders?"

Roderick winced, a guilty look on his impish face, but they all managed to say, "Yes, Mumsy!"

"That's good. See that you do." She cast a refined,

civilized smile at C+T and Co. and said, "Now. Let's see about getting you all out of here, shall we? I think it's time."

"Er … yes, ma'am." Pilot tipped his hat politely to her. "Thank you!"

"Run along now and play, all of you."

They hesitated for a moment. Until the Ghost of Mrs. Hecklestone, Proper Victorian Lady, turned back to that grumpy old doorknob and gave it a terrifying, ghoulish, Proper Victorian Piece of Her Mind!

"GAAAAHHHHH!!!!" they all screamed in horror as the nightmarish apparition exploded in a thrashing froth of ectoplasmic rage, and ran for the dining room as the plasma bulbs suddenly began firing again like they were trying to outdo the storm outside.

"Hurry!" Simon urged them, his voice strained and beginning to crackle with wild static. "I've poured on every ounce of mystical whiz-bangery I've got but I can't keep this up much longer! *Gnghh* …"

"Hold on, Speakie!" Cheryl shouted. "We're coming!"

Arms and legs windmilling wildly, Cheryl grabbed for him as she ran past. Then, together with Tweed, Artie, Pilot and Feedback, they dove straight for the glassy silver screen in front of them, reaching for the ghostly figures of the Hecklestone kids as they went. There was no hesitation—also, no crashing of glass, no shattering of shards—but just a weird, liquidy-cool sensation. The thunderstorm ended abruptly, almost as soon as they all tumbled through, out of the astral plane … and into the Drive-In parking lot.

Much to the astonishment of the car-bound, movie-watching patrons.

Cheryl glanced back in time to see Artie just make it through the shrinking portal. He was looking over his shoulder at Ramshackle—who suddenly vanished in a burst of the same golden light that swallowed them up. Cheryl heard Artie's cry of denial.

And then she heard one last thing as the portal began to fade from view. The creaking and shrieking of the old house grew even louder. But, in those last few moments, Cheryl thought it sounded more like a forlorn, lonely wailing than an angry howl.

15 THERE'S NO PLACE LIKE HOUSE

"**W**OW! That's the best 3D effect I've ever seen!" Cheryl heard the voice of Mr. Bottoms exclaim as she ran, crouched low, past a wood-panelled minivan, noisy with Bottoms boys in the back seats. "It's like those characters just leaped right off the screen! Of course, the plot didn't make a lick of sense ..."

It was awfully late for the Bottoms tots to be out and about. Then again, Mr. and Mrs. Bottoms had doubtless been unable to find a sitter that night and had brought John, Paul, George and Bingo along in the hopes they'd sleep through at least half of the double bill.

Talk about wishful thinking, Cheryl thought fleetingly as she dodged past the van.

The sudden cloudburst had lasted just long enough to help disguise the fact that there really had been *real* screen-leaping-offing and Cheryl breathed a sigh of relief that it wasn't enough rain to send any of their patrons packing. As the familiar smell of damp Drive-In lot gravel mixed with buttered popcorn wafted by, she couldn't keep the goofy grin from spreading across her face. She ducked and dodged and weaved between cars, a Drive-In speaker tucked under her arm and her cousin's dark-haired head in her sights, popping up like a gopher between the cars three rows in front of her.

"Psst!" she whispered. "Tweed! Wait up!"

She caught up to her a few seconds later and the two girls shared a quick hug—with bonus congratulatory back-patting—and a robust C+T Secret Signal (patent pending) before scuttling off to hide behind a hedge at the perimeter of the lot.

"We did it!" Tweed exclaimed in a triumphant monotone. "We're home!"

"We did! We are!" Cheryl nodded so enthusiastically her rain-damp pigtails spun like helicopter rotors. "Have you seen the others?"

"I think I saw the boys heading for the barn." Tweed hitched a thumb in the direction of C+T headquarters.

Cheryl's brow creased in a faint frown. "And ... the Hecks?"

Tweed silently shook her head.

"Oh."

"I mean ... we had a pretty good hold on them,

254

coming through the portal," Tweed said. "I felt that. So I *know* we got them out of the house at least."

"Yeah," Cheryl said. "I think so ..."

"Maybe Simon can spot them," Tweed suggested, nodding at the little metal box Cheryl still had tucked under her arm. "I mean ... if they're floating around here somewhere, his Spirit Stone might spot them, right?"

"Right! Good idea!" Cheryl lifted the speaker up in front of her face. "Hey!" she whispered loudly. "Speaker Boy!"

But there was no answer. And the Spirit Stone of Simon Omar was dull and dark and lifeless. Cheryl bit her lip to keep it from trembling.

"Speakie ...?"

Silence.

Tweed put a hand on her shoulder. "C'mon. Let's get to the barn."

Cheryl nodded, and carefully tucked the defunct speaker into her knapsack pocket. Staying as low to the ground as possible, the twins ran as fast as they could back to the barn. Pilot was standing at the door, with an enormous grin plastered to his mug. Feedback was there, too—looking just a little stunned, but otherwise hale and hearty and whole.

And ... so, too, were the Hecklestone Three!

Daphne, Roderick and Edwina stood in a tight knot in the middle of the big old barn, gazing around in wonder and amazement. Roddy seemed particularly fascinated with the Moviemobile—his eyes were practically glued to the shiny red car—and little Eddy was chewing furiously on her baby finger, as if to make sure that it was really there and chewable. Daphne just stood and bounced in place, her ringlets jiggling. And there wasn't even one little spot of them that was the least bit see-through. They were every bit as flesh and blood as the twins and their friends.

"Holy moly!" Cheryl cried.

"Outstanding!" Tweed yelped, dropping her signature monotone in her excitement.

"Hooray for the magic of the movies, right, ladies?" Pilot was grinning from ear to ear.

"Now *that's* what I call an awesome 3D experience!" Cheryl exclaimed. "I mean, literally!"

There was a chaotic moment of hugging and high-fiving—with varying degrees of success and Victorian variations—between the twins and the Three. Then a flood of melancholy momentarily washed over Cheryl.

She sighed. "If only Simon Omar was here to see this," she said quietly, and blinked at the prickling behind her eyes.

"I am!" said a familiar voice from behind her.

Cheryl nearly jumped out of her sneakers and spun to grab wildly for the speaker in her knapsack. But when she hauled the contraption out and held it up, the ruby-red jewel was still dark. She frowned in confusion and heard Tweed snort in what sounded like amusement. Which didn't seem particularly sensitive in that moment ... until she felt a tapping on her shoulder.

Slowly Cheryl raised her eyes ...

"Gah!!" she exclaimed and fumbled with the speaker, dropping it into the white-gloved hands of the tall, slender gentleman wearing a natty tuxedo and a wacky grin standing right in front of her.

Even without his bejewelled mystic turban, it was, quite obviously, Simon Omar, World-famous Wizard of the West End!

"TA-DAA!" he exclaimed with a flourish, confirming it. "Look at me! I'm ... I'm *me* again! I'm corporeal! Unexploded!"

Cheryl threw herself at him in a spontaneous hug, joined an instant later by Tweed.

"Yes, yes." Simon patted them on their shoulders. "All right. You girls—and you lads—you really *are* magicians of the highest order!" He pushed them gently to arm's length, smiling. "Now tell me. Where does one procure a mystic's turban in this town?"

A babble of excited chatter erupted, but suddenly Tweed looked around. "Wait." She frowned worriedly. "Where's Shrimpcake?"

Before anyone could answer, a rain-bedraggled Artie suddenly burst through the door, gasping for breath.

"Artie!" Cheryl exclaimed.

"Where've you been, Art-Bart?" Pilot asked.

"I wound up over on the far side of the Drive-In," Artie huffed. "Near the mini-golf range … *huff* … *huff* … so I cut through there and circled back around. My new shoes are gonna need a shine. But, best of all, look who I found!" He pointed overhead and a wobbly-looking, slightly singed gargoyle, carrying a golf club, flapped unsteadily in through the overhead hayloft door.

"Ramshackle!" Tweed cried.

"My putter!" Cheryl said. "It must have acted as a lodestone for Ramshackle the same way the tungsten projector thingamabob did for us!"

"Yup," Artie said, grinning. "I found him perched on the Castle Putt-sylvania hole, along with the foam-rubber gargoyles. He likes it there and wants to know if he can stay."

"Of course he can!" Tweed exclaimed. "It's a properly Gothic home for him, after all."

"Hey …" Pilot scratched at his nose, thinking. "Speaking of which … Mr. Omar … where are *you* going to live? I mean you—and the Hecks—you'll all need a place to live now."

"Of course they will," Tweed said, her grey eyes lighting with a sudden flash of inspiration. "And there's a perfectly good—perfectly *empty*—house not more than a few miles from here! On Eerie Lane!"

Cheryl knew instantly where Tweed was going with that and her blue eyes sparkled with excitement as she nodded in agreement. "More than enough room for a retired magician freshly arrived from abroad," she said, grinning, "*and* his three adopted children, don't you think?"

"W-what?!" Artie sputtered. "Didn't we all just bust our backsides getting them *out* of that place?"

"Sure! But that was before they had backsides of their own!" Cheryl waved a hand at the erstwhile mystic and ex-departed Hecklestone kids. "I mean, corporeally speaking."

"You girls make a good point," Simon said, frowning thoughtfully. "Now that we're no longer spectres, I think we'd prove more than a match for the Hecklestone House."

Pilot was grinning. "You'll have to come up with a cover story—Wiggins doesn't get a whole lotta newcomers—but it could work …"

"Of course it could! I am a performer. A magician. I'm an expert at making my audience believe what I tell them." Simon turned to Daphne, Roddy and Eddy. "That is, if that's all right with you three?"

"Oh, it is!" Daphne exclaimed.

"I say!" Roddy nodded. "Capital idea!"

"I'd like that," Edwina said with a serious look on her small face. "When we left, I think the house was very sad to see us go. Maybe it's not *that* naughty after all. Maybe it was just afraid to be left alone."

Cheryl remembered the forlorn cry she'd heard as they'd tumbled through the mirror portal and thought that Edwina might be right about that.

"And anyway," the little ex-ghost continued, "it would be awfully nice to sleep in my own bed again— instead of just hovering over it ..."

"All right, then!" Simon clapped his gloved hands together and gathered the kids, shooing them toward the barn door like a mother hen with chicks. "It's settled. Now, you'll have to promise to behave yourselves ..."

"Let's not be hasty, sir!" Roderick protested.

"First things first," Daphne said as she went. "I think a few renovations might be in order. Like, say, a new front doorknob!"

"Sure!" Cheryl called out. "And maybe a few choice movie posters in your bedroom to go with all those old photos!"

"And I'll swing by tomorrow to give you a hand repairing the hole I put in the roof!" Pilot said, grinning.

"And we'll come get our bikes," Tweed said. "And maybe give that hedge a trim."

Cheryl nodded, smiling, and refrained from mentioning the potential presence of hedge spiders.

The gaggle of ex-spectres said their goodbyes and their thank-yous, waving as they walked off into the night, leaving behind a slightly dazed, exhausted, giddy-with-success quintet of kids surrounded by the warmth and familiarity and blissful non-hauntedness of the big old barn.

"I think I'm gonna go home now," Feedback said finally. "Maybe spend some time cleaning my room. Play some video games. Re-evaluate my previously held world view. Y'know ... stuff like that."

"Karl?" Cheryl stopped him. "You won't ... tell anyone about all this, right?"

Feedback laughed a little wildly. "Who on earth would believe me?" he asked. "They'd think I was as nutty as you two!"

The girls exchanged a wry glance.

"Hey," he said. "You guys can be as nutty as you want. Wiggins folk might think it's weird, but I think it's pretty darn cool. Thanks for the real-life adventure!"

"I'd better get going, too," Artie said, putting out an arm for Ramshackle to perch on. "My mom's starting to think I'm a vampire in real life with all these late nights."

"Wait until she sees you in those duds!" Pilot said. "That'll confirm the suspicion. C'mon, Karl. We can all walk home together."

Cheryl and Tweed walked them all to the door and peeked out.

"Credits are rolling." Cheryl nodded at the screen. "How apropos."

Tweed grinned wearily. "I guess we should go back to the farmhouse and tell Pops the sleepover was a bust."

"And give him a nice big hug!" Cheryl agreed. "And do extra chores this week."

"Lots of 'em," Tweed said.

"Yeah," Pilot agreed. "You should. That was a dumb thing you two did." He held up a hand to forestall outbursts. "An *awesome* dumb thing. You guys just gave those kids and that exploded magician a chance at being a family."

Cheryl blushed and shrugged. "Aw, never mind. We couldn't have done it without you guys."

"Of course not!" Artie said. "Together we're the League of Awesome!"

"And the stars of our very own movie!" Tweed said, thrusting her hand out in a fist. The others gathered around and did the same, knuckles touching, arms splayed in a circle like the spokes of a film reel.

Cheryl grinned. "Camera's rolling …"

Tweed grinned back. "Aaaaand …"

Pilot sighed indulgently, expecting another ACTION!! sequence.

Artie saved him with a cry of "BEDTIME!!" and ran off into the night.

Cheryl and Tweed watched him go. Then they turned to each other, and as the screen faded to black and the cars in the Drive-In lot revved up their engines, they gave each other one last C+T Secret Signal (patent pending) before they shuffled off toward the little white farmhouse, past the Starlight Paradise double screens, glad to already be in the place that they called home.

ACKNOWLEDGMENTS

CUE '80s MONTAGE THANK-YOU SOUNDTRACK!

Aaaaand ... ACTION!!

We are thrilled to once again have the opportunity to thank all of the wonderful, talented, hard-working people who have made it possible for us to tell tales of the Wiggins Weird!

Steven Burley, storyboard artist extraordinaire, who continues to amaze and delight and befuddle and confound and make us slightly barfy from laughing so hard. We can't thank him enough!

Huge thanks to our extraordinary agents, Jessica Regel and Tara Hart, charter members of the League of Awesome—along with the fantastic folks at Puffin,

Penguin Canada, especially Lynne Missen, our amazing editor; Sandra Tooze, our production editor; Catherine Dorton, our copy editor; and Vikki Vansickle, publicist extraordinaire—you guys really are superheroes! Your LoA rings are in the mail!

Thank you, as always, to Jean Naggar and the staff of JVNLA. And to the fine folks at Foundry Literary.

Thanks to our families, especially—as always—our moms. We salute you with the L+J Secret Signal (patent pending)!

But our biggest thanks goes out to all our honorary Wigginsians—you guys!—for helping to make the first book a success! We hope you enjoy the continuing adventures of Cheryl and Tweed and Company!

W-O-W!!